THE MALEFIC NATION

GRAHAM'S RESOLUTION, BOOK 4

A. R. SHAW

APOCALYPTIC VENTURES, LLC

Dedicated to my son, Adam
You can do anything you set your mind to.

1

Instant

"Up and at 'em, Bang," Graham whispered to the sleepy boy from his pallet on the floor. Bang's eyes fluttered in the low light that seeped through the sheet-covered window. Sheriff, who'd slept at the foot of Macy's bed at the cabin, did so here as well; but now he rested on the rotting wood floor next to her feet.

Graham didn't trust that anyone in the room was actually asleep. In the last few days they had all existed only on the margin of sleep, rarely dipping over to the other side because of utter fear and the shock of recent events.

No, the sleepers had heard every word. They'd been through this routine: they were only biding their time, waiting for those who'd awakened to leave the room so that they might approach the edge of slumber once again.

As Bang stirred, Graham tugged on his boots and turned his attention to his other side, where Tala rested. He tucked his end of the cover around her back to keep the warmth in. Cool morning air crept through the cracks in the flooring. This was a blessing in the heat of midday, but a shivering curse at sunrise. Graham bent down and brushed his lips against Tala's bare shoulder, then pulled the blanket higher. He'd worried that she'd get sick from the mold in this chilly, rain-soaked old house, but that no longer mattered; they were leaving today. Now he worried where they would sleep tonight.

Graham looped his belt around the waist of his jeans while Bang sat up and rubbed his eyes, smashing his fists into them in a circular motion. Sheriff arose as well and lowered his front end, stretching his back, and shaking his tail out. "Come on, let's go," Graham whispered again. To which of them he spoke didn't matter; they would both follow him out of the quiet room, Bang silent as a phantom, Sheriff with the clacking of his nails along the weathered floor.

"Good morning, Graham," Olivia said as she bent over the propane stove. "It's instant coffee for now on; make yourself a cup." She motioned with her hand toward the far end of the makeshift table where she'd set up a thermos, the kind that had a pump you pushed until coffee poured out in a welcome river. But hot water came rushing out instead; it looked nothing like the dark, rich coffee that Graham expected.

Olivia watched his confused state; clearly he'd never made instant coffee before, probably never had to. "Mix in a heaping spoonful of the coffee crystals," she said as Graham stood transfixed.

The heat began to radiate through his cup, alerting the pain sensors in his hand enough to want to set it down. If the alarm were in the form of brewed coffee, he'd ignore the threat of a first-degree burn, no matter how hot it was, because the prospect of coffee negated first-degree burns. But boiling water did not, so Graham set the cup down. Olivia stared at him as he picked up the canister of coffee crystal. "Just one heaping teaspoon," she repeated, and Graham wasn't sure if it was a rationing thing or if she was trying to anticipate how this new procedure would digress into a disruption of their typical morning routine since they were obviously out of the real stuff. In any event, he didn't appreciate being the guinea pig. He scooped out a spoonful and stirred it into the water. It turned the clear hot water into brown hot water with a smell only vaguely reminiscent of coffee.

"See, that wasn't so hard," Olivia said. Graham had a slight impulse to punch her, and he realized that this was not like him. He hoped, for her sake, that there was actually caffeine in this pale brown fluid.

"You can add sweetener, but we're out of creamer, I'm afraid," she reminded him.

Graham raised the cup to his face, just to smell the aroma at first. "I think I'll take it black," he said, then took a sip. It came back to him: he'd had instant coffee before; he only remembered it when the bitter tang hit him. And then, as if it were only yesterday, he saw the young brunette woman approaching him in a grocery store with one of those convenient built-in Starbucks carts with the cup holders attached, where you could pay five dollars for a mocha to sip as you combed the store's aisles for a box of K-Cups that would cost you fifty cents each. She'd appeared out of nowhere in the signature green apron, carrying a tray of tiny caffeine jolts. She offered him a swig from two cups only big enough for munchkins and asked him if he could tell which one was Pike Place and which one was the new Viva coffee. Not one to turn down free coffee, Graham had tasted both and immediately knew which one was the new roast. It had a slightly bitter taste—not bad bitter, not bitter like the fluid burning his right hand at the moment, but not particularly pleasant.

Graham took another swig as he followed Bang and Sheriff out to the front porch, tipping his cup in thanks to Olivia. He swallowed the bitter brew and flashed back to the look on the brunette's face when he had announced the losing Starbuck's candidate; she turned in disappointment, maybe even taking offense, and approached the next potential taster. Was he supposed to say the Viva wasn't bad? In truth, it wasn't awful, but it wasn't as good as the Pike Place.

Graham stared at the chestnut imposter in his hand. *What I wouldn't give for some of that Viva about now.* Still, the thought didn't keep him from downing the remainder in the cup he was holding. "Ugh, time to quit," he said. "Nothing's worth *this*."

Crumpling the empty cup, he surveyed the day before him. From the rickety porch he could see that fog had settled in. Foggy weather tended to make everyone a little edgy. Bang had already released the chickens from the crates and scattered feed on the ground. While Bang gathered kindling, Sheriff sat at attention, mesmerized by the birds. Graham had no doubt he'd make a meal of them if he ever became hungry enough, and the fact that he seemed to protect them from Elsa and Frank, the Belgian shepherds, amazed him. But the other dogs had learned from Sheriff that these particular birds were part of their pack, and others often marveled at the dogs lazing about as chickens foraged between them.

Elsa and Frank were bigger than Sheriff, but he had quickly managed to become the alpha. At times Graham wasn't sure if the dogs regarded themselves as pets or guards of these strange people they now found themselves with. Either was fine with him; the dogs had done their fair share of protecting, and it was no secret that their human counterparts could use any help they could get.

"Hey Graham," Sam said, stepping up onto the far side of the old porch with Addy alongside him.

"Good morning. You ready to head out today?" Graham's hands had been scalding only minutes ago, but now he rubbed them together to fend off the chill.

"You bet. This fog is a good cover for us—well, for both sides, I guess." Sam's mouth turned into a slight frown.

Addy eyed Bang gathering kindling and turned to her father. The man nodded at her, but as a warning he made a sign, pointing two fingers to his eyes and then waving them in a circle, finishing with a point in her direction: *Don't leave my sight.* Addy scampered off with a wide grin on her face, and Bang looked up when she approached him, holding out her arms to indicate that she would share the load. At one time, they couldn't get these two anywhere near each other, but now they couldn't keep them apart. Wherever Bang was Addy would be, and vice versa.

"Who's still asleep?" Sam asked.

Sam's impatience was contagious, and it made Graham feel guilty.

He knew they were leaving to head north this morning, but now he, too, wanted to get going; no one ever trusted fog. It was blind faith: you had to believe something was there or it wasn't, and as a math man, Graham trusted neither.

"Tala and the twins. I think Rick and Mark too. I'm not sure, there's several more. Dalton, Clarisse, Lucy, and McCann are on watch." A smell of fake maple syrup wafted on the cool morning air, and voices emanated from inside.

"No one really sleeps anymore," Sam said. "They'll be up soon. I think I'll grab some coffee. Be right back. Watch Addy for me a sec?"

"Will do."

Graham thought to warn Sam about the coffee, but gave up; java seemed like a pretty low priority in the grand scheme of things. Instead, he turned to the children stacking the kindling they'd managed to find. "This enough, Graham?" Bang asked, standing next to a teetering pile of sticks.

"That'll do, buddy. You two come get cleaned up and get breakfast after you round up the hens." He watched as the two kids cleverly sprinkled feed into the wire crates, tricking the chickens to enter. A few were wise to this hoax by now, and the kids were left with finding a way to herd them in.

Graham scanned the perimeter out front. The visibility would be an issue driving out; the fog would either help them or haunt them, but they would find out soon enough.

The radio unit inside the cabin clicked twice, meaning all was well from the watch positions. Sam returned with his cup of faux joe. "Instant," he said, raising the cup in front of him and taking another sip of the steamy liquid. "But better than nothin'."

"Yeah," Graham agreed. At this point, he thought a second bitter cup might actually be necessary. The fog was making him apprehensive, and anything that might increase his awareness held appeal, no matter the bitter taste.

2

On the Move

"Okay group, I've called this quick meeting to get us going in a timely manner this morning," said Dalton. Everyone—pack your bags. Then manage your other assigned tasks—from Bang getting the chickens in their place to Reuben gassing up the trucks. Any questions?"

"I need to examine the injured before we set out," Clarisse said, her hand raised.

"Really?" Dalton was a little exasperated with the bandages, antibacterial ointment, and medications she kept applying or pumping into him.

Clarisse dropped her arm in frustration. "Yes, Dalton; *especially* you." She then called out, "McCann, Tala, Sam, and Rick as well."

"I'm not *injured*. Just pointing that out," Tala interjected.

"Of course not Tala—sorry. Anyone else needing medical attention before we head out, see me after. This is the time to tell me about blisters, boils, lice—whatever you've got, bring it to me." A chuckle erupted around the room before she continued. "In all seriousness, don't tell me you need medical attention when we're on the road and all our supplies are packed up. Now's the time."

No one else spoke up, so Dalton clapped his hand to his thigh and said, "All right. Everyone get to work. I want to be out of here in twenty minutes, tops. Oh, and everyone do your business before we leave. We're not stopping for potty breaks."

The crowd in the main room dispersed, leaving only the injured and Clarisse along with her large tackle box full of medical supplies.

"I'll meet with you last, Tala," she said. Tala smiled and wandered off to use the restroom, taking the potty warning seriously.

"Let's start with McCann since he's the least injured," Clarisse said, opening up her first aid supplies. She adjusted her stethoscope around her neck and said, "Let's see it. Take off your shirt."

"It sounds so inappropriate when you say it like that," Rick joked. "He's only a boy, for Christ's sake."

McCann chuckled, but Clarisse was not amused. "Shut up," she said to Rick without breaking concentration.

"Don't mess with her today, Rick," Dalton warned.

McCann unbuttoned his shirt and slid his injured arm out of the sleeve while Dalton sat nearby.

"That still looks bad," Dalton said.

"Does everyone have to watch?" McCann asked.

Clarisse examined the pink scar tissue over the gunshot wound in McCann's shoulder. "Actually, it looks pretty good. There's no infection, and it's healing well. And I want you to keep it covered day and night. I know it's still tender, but the wound will toughen in time. Any questions?" she asked.

"Nope, I'm good," McCann said, eager to get his shirt back on.

"I know you don't like to take it, but if you took some ibuprofen it would lessen some of the swelling and ease the pain. It's going to be a long day."

"No ma'am, thank you," McCann simply said in response.

"Okay. I want you to stay and help with these guys. Watch and learn, in other words. Next?" Clarisse called out.

Sam came forward before the others had a chance. "I've got stuff to do, so let's get this over with," he said, dropping his pants without being told. He exposed his left inner thigh to the stitched gash he'd sustained when they'd fled the besieged prepper camp.

Clarisse knew he was embarrassed because his face turned shades of pink behind his beard, but he was making the best of the situation. He turned his one leg out, showing a bandage that covered his stitches. Clarisse replaced her gloves and then looked at him before she touched the injury. "What is this goo?"

"It's honey," Sam said.

"Honey? I didn't tell you to put honey on your injury. Look Sam, I know you like to do things your own way, but you could have introduced a secondary infection to your wound with this stuff. Where did you get it?"

McCann and the others were silent. Getting chewed out in front of your buddies by Clarisse was never fun.

"Is it infected?" Sam said calmly.

"No, it looks pretty good, actually."

"Then don't worry about it."

"What if the honey had botulism spores?" Clarisse asked.

"I boiled it before I applied it."

She huffed out a breath. "Look, I know studies showed honey is a great substitute for antibacterial ointment, but we have sufficient supplies of the ointment. You don't need to resort to honey—not yet. Are you still taking the antibiotics?"

"Yes."

"Got any great backups for that?" Clarisse asked with an unnecessary degree of attitude.

"Not exactly," Sam said. "But there are other alternatives."

"We have modern medicine for now, Sam. Let's stick with the tried and true while we still have it. When we run out, we'll use other methods and risk new complications," she said, rebandaging the wound. "We'll leave the stitches in for a few more days. That was a serious wound, and you can't afford an infection right now."

"Got it," Sam said, pulling up his pants.

"Dalton, you're up."

"Rick's going next," Dalton said, his voice serious.

Clarisse looked at him, ready to challenge his authority, but Dalton gave her a stern look. He wasn't happy with her treatment of Sam, she suspected, but that couldn't be helped. She knew it was wrong to undermine Sam in front of everyone—especially McCann—and she probably deserved Dalton's disapproval, but she couldn't let Sam utilize his own means of healing without at least consulting her first.

"Okay then, Rick, you're next."

"Mine's not nearly as interesting," he said, sitting down.

"Any concussion is serious, Rick." Clarisse held up a pen for Rick to follow with his eyes as she waved it from side to side. "Any dizziness, nausea, or headaches?"

"No."

"Sleeping okay?"

"No one is sleeping okay," Rick said, as if she had made a joke.

Clarisse pressed around the wound slightly. Green bruising spread out at the base of Rick's skull, where shrapnel from an arterial blast had hit him. "Everything looks good, it's nicely scabbed over. Let's look at your shin now. Any issues?"

"It just itches; I'm trying not to scratch it," Rick said.

"That's normal—it's healing well—but try not to scratch off the scabs. I'd say you were lucky twice."

Rick's face turned serious. Even though she hadn't intended to, Clarisse had reminded him of Steven's death again, in a spilt-second bringing Rick back to one of their greatest losses. If she hadn't felt bad for giving Sam a hard time about the alternative medicine, she was miserable now for reminding Rick of Steven's death. *Damn, I can't do anything right today.*

"Let me know if anything changes. Keep taking the anti-inflammatory for swelling," Clarisse said, and Rick recovered his pant leg and set off to work.

While McCann noted Rick's condition on the iPad she kept their medical records in, Clarisse washed her hands again and donned another pair of gloves.

Dalton approached and pulled up his army-green T-shirt. Clarisse knew he was upset with her, so she turned to McCann, silently signaling, *I think I can handle this one, and Tala's next. You go ahead and pack up.*

"You sure?" McCann asked.

"Yep," she said, knowing she was in for one of Dalton's lectures. "Please have Tala come in about ten minutes."

After getting his head out of the T-shirt, Dalton gingerly pulled the sleeve over his bandaged shoulder. Clarisse pulled off the taped bandages, taking care not to yank out any of Dalton's chest hairs. He watched her but said nothing.

"Go ahead, say it."

"Say what?" he asked.

"Why am I such a bitch?" she said.

"I wasn't going to say that, but since you asked, why *are* you such a bitch this morning?"

Clarisse looked into Dalton's face; she hadn't noticed that he now held her by the waist to steady her as she stood on her toes to inspect and redress his shoulder wound.

"I guess I'm just worried about everyone. We have serious injuries and a pregnant woman with us, and we don't know where we're going to sleep tonight. And we can't stay here."

"I know you don't do well with change, Clarisse, but we have to leave and regroup. We're not far enough away. There will be more resources in Hope, and we can give Tala a chance to have the baby and give ourselves time to heal and come up with a plan to return."

She looked away, and Dalton gave her waist a little shake. "We *will* come back, Clarisse. We'll get rid of them somehow, and we'll make it safe again."

She nodded, even though she doubted his words, and Dalton pulled her near to kiss her on the forehead. "Now, do you have any of Sam's honey? I hear it works better than this goop."

Clarisse snickered and shook her head, adding, "I'm such an idiot."

"No, you're just worried. We all are. Now, let's hurry up and get out of here," Dalton said, slipping his T-shirt back on.

There was a light rap on the doorframe, and then Tala's voice: "Are you ready for me Clarisse?"

Clarisse turned to the door, and behind Tala, she could see trucks being loaded and moved into position. They would leave here soon. "Yes, come in," she said as Dalton exited.

Tala held one hand on her belly as she walked nearer to Clarisse.

"Everything okay?" Clarisse asked.

"I think so. We're all a little edgy this morning," Tala said.

"Yeah." Clarisse nodded as she held the stethoscope to Tala's swollen belly. Hearing the baby's steady cadence, she smiled. "Sounds perfect." She then slipped a wireless blood pressure cuff over Tala's arm while holding her cell phone.

"Well, that's one I haven't seen before," Tala remarked. "Is that your phone?"

Clarisse held it up, "Yeah. I have an app on here for blood pressure calculations. Of course, it's worthless as a cell phone now, but I still use the app for this blood pressure cuff. The cuff eats up batteries, so I don't use it often, but for this trip I thought it would come in handy without having to open up all of the medical supplies." As the cuff squeezed Tala's arm, Clarisse watched for the pressure to fall within the normal range.

"How do you keep the cell phone batteries charged?" Tala asked.

Clarisse held up this little device with a hand crank attached to it. "I use this nifty gadget Rick gave me. You plug in the USB and then depress this in your palm over and over until it charges the phone. Actually, it takes a while, so I gave it to the boys—to charge both the phone and the iPad. Anything to keep those guys busy and out of trouble." She laughed, then looked directly at Tala. "Since you're well past the twenty-week mark, we need to keep track of your blood pressure. Of course, we're all bound to hit the limits these days."

Tala smiled. "I'm putting my trust in Hope. I think we'll find a safe place to rest a while."

"Aren't you worried about not having the baby in the United States?" Clarisse asked. No one else had mentioned it, but she knew they were all thinking how significant that was.

Tala took in a deep breath, then let it out. "No, I'm not worried about it. This baby is American because *we're* American. Just because we have to have it in another place doesn't change who the child is. Besides, I don't think we can really think in those terms anymore; with so few people left, I don't think borders hold the same significance they used to. There may not even *be* borders anymore, though we'll see soon enough, I guess.

"We're putting distance between us and a danger to our survival. We'll come back to confront that danger at a later date, because we know it's a cancer that must be dealt with. That's how I feel, at least. Dalton may have other ideas. You have to remember, I'm Native American. My people are from this continent, and"—she pointed a finger at Clarisse and smiled—"to my ancestors *you* were the trespassers on our land who came in and set the borders."

Clarisse nodded. "I didn't think of it that way."

"Invaders never do." Tala chuckled, shaking her head.

"Okay Pocahontas, any complaints? Physically, I mean?"

"None," Tala said.

"Great. Please make sure you drink plenty of water. I know that's a problem when we don't stop very often, but we can't afford for you to get a urinary tract infection. Please tell me if anything concerns you," Clarisse said, stressing this statement because she knew Tala didn't like to complain.

"You ladies ready?" Graham asked from the doorway. "We're all loaded up."

"I think so," Tala said as Graham helped her down the rickety porch steps.

"Hurry up, or they'll leave you behind," Graham warned Clarisse with a smile.

Clarisse picked up her medical satchel and looked behind her to see if they'd forgotten anything. She wondered how many people had taken refuge here in this old, weathered cabin. The back door stood open, as it had before they'd arrived. Animals would once again inhabit this refuge, reclaiming as their own this shelter from the wind and rain until the wood rotted completely through and back to the earth.

Her boot steps thudded as she made her way out. She absent-mindedly began to shut the door, but then remembered to leave it ajar. *Sanctuary*, she said to herself.

3

Foreign

They headed south to the end of the road through the fog, at a slow pace along the narrow fire and logging roads until the dirt gave way to pavement once again. Dalton and Rick led the caravan of five vehicles.

McCann and Macy drove a truck loaded down with supplies and the crates of chickens, pulling as quietly as possible a horse trailer that they had managed to find back in Cascade. Bang sat between them in the cab, as tall as he could to glimpse the view through the windshield. They were the fourth vehicle in line; Reuben and his wife drove the last supply truck and kept an eye on the end of the line, as well as behind them for anyone trailing their escape.

The day seemed too much like a fall camping trip except that the unknown had everyone on edge. Dalton radioed for a relay check after ten minutes, and each driver called in with no signs of trouble. Graham drove the second truck, carrying three dogs, Tala, and most of the children. Sam drove the fourth, which was more of a camper that included a kitchen and most of the rest of the displaced residents within.

"Graham, we're going to scout ahead a ways to check things out," Rick said. "There are so many bends in this road, and with the low visibility in this fog I want to make sure the coast is clear and that we're not running into any setups. You keep your speed steady and wait for our message."

"Copy. By the way, did you guys hear the new national radio message? Over."

Rick held the microphone. He wasn't sure he wanted to hear any radio message being broadcast over the new Islamic national radio waves. "No, I guess we didn't yet. Over."

"Let's just say you can't unhear it once you do. Pretty disturbing. Over."

"Can't wait. Back in ten. Rick out."

Rick looked at Dalton, who had locked his steely vision northward. "Do you want to hear the new message?" Rick asked.

"Dammit," Dalton grumbled, switching on the truck's radio. In the past they had often turned on the receiver only to hear a recorded message repeatedly warning them to keep the documents of the Constitution below ground until an adequate population rose again, or the one telling people to care for one another and live peacefully. The message regarding contamination from the virus didn't apply to them anymore, but it did to other survivors. They had listened to these messages repeatedly even though they dated from right before the end of the world as they knew it.

The radio crackled to its familiar beeps, followed by an unwelcome voice in broken English: "This is the Islamic State of America. The infidels are dead." The message then switched into what Dalton knew as Arabic. He'd heard enough already, and he turned off the noise, returning his vision to the road ahead. With the heavy silence that followed, Rick and Dalton reaffirmed their goal: to escape, leaving behind the malefic intrusion into their once free nation.

4

Ideas

Dalton sped through several winding curves, ahead of the rest of the group, but he and Rick found nothing out of the ordinary. Abandoned homesteads lay scattered in a ghostly existence; every gas station was devoid of humans, but in their absence wildlife and the spread of forest undergrowth were a telling reminder that things were no longer as they once had been—and would never be again. Eventually they slowed down and waited for the others to catch up.

"Reuben, this is Dalton. Everything clear back there? Over."

"Affirmative," came Reuben's voice. "We're clear. Over."

Dalton held the microphone to his chest and drove on, not sure what to say next. The persistent fog was finally breaking up, the sun burning off what was left of the opaque blindness. With their path now laid bare before them, it was as if they were being shown the way —or led astray. Dalton wasn't sure which.

"Looks like the fog is clearing up here. Keep a lookout behind us, though. Over." Dalton switched off the radio.

Rick hadn't said a thing for a number of miles, instead staring out the passenger side window. This silence always bothered Dalton; Rick could be like a sulking child sometimes. He knew his buddy was still mourning, but he needed him now; he needed him to think. Dalton checked his rearview mirror and saw that the rest of the caravan was catching up with them. When he looked back at Rick, he couldn't take it anymore. "Rick, what's on your mind?"

Rick looked forward, a bit annoyed at having his concentration interrupted. "Nothing," he finally said, his hands held out before him. "What makes you think I've got something on my mind?"

Dalton had figured he'd do this. "Rick, I've known you too long. You always have *something* on your mind. Now, out with it."

Rick adjusted himself in the seat. "You *think* you know me . . ." he began. "All right look, they're fucking *everywhere*. How are we going to defeat that? We have access to supplies, man, but we need bombs and endless artillery to push them out. I . . . I was thinking, hit them with EMPs. They're using all of our own technology. If we can get our hands on the equipment, we could make several small ones and . . ."

Dalton thought about the idea—the implications and the potential aftermath. "Where in the hell would we get that many capacitors? And"—Dalton shook his head—"you could only make little ones. Look, it's a start, but not good enough. You forget two things. First, we can't defeat them block by block. The size of the electromagnetic pulse you're talking about, we'd need an endless supply of them. Second, they *want* to live in the sixth century. Sure, they're using some of our equipment to aid their invasion, but they're about oppression, slavery, and some twisted idea of turning the globe back to ancient times. They don't give a damn about electricity and technology.

"I'm afraid that would be playing right into their hands. We'd be doing them a favor. We need technology to defeat them. I don't know how or what, yet, but I think we'd regret setting off a bunch of little EMPs over our own country. To set a large one off we'd need a nuke, and hell, the country wouldn't be worth coming back to if we had to go that route."

"Yeah, okay." Rick dropped his hand in a defeated gesture and went back to staring out the window, trying to come up with something else. The evergreen trees rushed by, and occasionally there were glimpses of the Skagit River.

"No," Dalton continued. "There are very few of us now, and a whole lot of them. The answer is somewhere; we'll figure it out once we get everyone safely to Hope. We'll regroup. Tala can have the baby, and we'll come up with something." He nodded, as if to reassure himself as much as Rick.

"Yeah, we need some kind of selective . . . *bomb* or something," Rick mumbled.

"There's no such thing, I'm afraid." The dilemma stuck with Dalton; if they were ever to return, everything hinged on purging the land of the jihadists once and for all.

After another expanse of silence-filled minutes, Dalton broke the trance. "Where the hell are we, by the way? You're the navigator. This winding road is making me nervous. How much longer until we can turn off Highway 20?"

Rick ruffled the paper map on his lap, identical to those kept in the other vehicles and marked the same way. "Well, remember how we took back roads getting to the cabin and stayed off Highway 20 as much as possible? We even took Ranger Station to Powerline and came back out on Clark Cabin to Highway 20. Then we took Forest Service 1060 after we crossed Bacon Creek to the north and slipped up into the old cabin off Hope Lane. There were no accessible roads north through the Cascades, so we're back down to Highway 20. Our plan is to make it over to Ross Lake."

"That's our first stop. We'll try and see if there's a boat that can take us all across, Reuben said there was a barge there a year ago that they were using to repair Ross Dam. The Skagit connects Diablo to Ross Lake. Reuben knows of some cabins near there, and I'm hoping we can spend the night in them. Tomorrow we'll head up the road from the north end of Ross Lake and cross into Canada at the lake's northern tip. The only road out is Silver Creek, on the Canadian end of Ross Lake; it meanders up to Hope."

"Okay, that's the plan, then. We may have to ditch some vehicles," Dalton said.

"Yeah, we have a contingency worked out if it comes to that."

"Let's hope it doesn't. We still have a long way to go and I'd prefer not to lose anyone else along the way," Dalton as they approached the first of a few darkened mountain tunnels they'd have to go through. He slowed their approach, and they looked for any sign of the terrorists.

They drove through the darkness, and Dalton slowed when they neared the end of the tunnel, cautiously creeping out into the unknown. But no ambush awaited them, no hidden forces—nothing.

The road wound endlessly through forests of evergreens and cypress trees, crisscrossing the Skagit River, until they found themselves along a cliff's steep edge overlooking an expanse of vivid teal-blue water.

"Is that Ross Lake?" Rick asked, "The water is incredibly blue."

Dalton slowed their truck to an easy stop. "No, this is Diablo Lake. God, it's been so long; I haven't been here since I was a boy. Ross is about four miles up to the northeast, connected to Diablo by the Skagit. Let me check with Reuben, but the map says to turn here." He switched on his microphone. "Reuben, the map says to turn left here at the base of Diablo. Ross is farther up, right? Over."

After a few seconds hesitation, Reuben answered. "That's right. The last time I was here, a few years back, you had to cross the Diablo Dam and park behind it. They took us by water taxi from Diablo through the inlet and into Ross Lake to the cabin resort after that. They were in the process of fixing up Diablo Dam when the world fell apart. There should still be a small barge here that we can use to get the vehicles upriver. Otherwise, there are no roads on this side of the border that lead to the other side. There's only one road out, and that's on Canada's side. Over."

"Thanks, Reuben. Dalton out."

"Hmmm, sounds defensible," Rick said.

"Don't get any ideas. It's still not far enough," Dalton said, aiming left to drive over the dam. Then he picked up the microphone and addressed them all: "Keep your eyes open. Stay vigilant. I doubt they've made it this far yet, but we're exposed until we get across the border." The hairs on Dalton's neck rose. He knew they were taking a big risk, and he only hoped that the jihadists didn't have the time or the men to track them down yet. Going to Canada only bought them a little time. Radio broadcasts indicated the jihadists intended to spread over all lands, but conquering the United States was their first priority. White cast iron lamps lined the top of the dam, flanking the driveway—a design from times past. He wondered if the lamps sprung to life as the darkness fell, filling the void at night with courage, or if they, too, had been snuffed out like most of humanity.

Rick had his weapon at the ready, and both of them checked everywhere for movement in the shadows. Dalton felt as if doubt and fear were creeping up his spine. If he were the jihadists, he'd take their whole group out from the cliffs above, easily picking them off one vehicle at a time. Or he'd simply blow the whole dam up once they were all on it.

Debris from past storms was scattered on the highway in areas where the snow had piled high and then melted. Rocks from the cliffs above had fallen; no road crews had come to sweep them away. There were no tire tracks, no tourists' refuse, no human footsteps evident here. Yet as they drove through the dam gate, the roadway was pristine. There was not a shred of refuse to be seen, and Dalton's senses bristled upon seeing the marked difference.

"We're all on now," Rick said, his voice seeming as tense as Dalton's nerves.

"We've just pulled off," Dalton said, knowing Rick had his eyes behind them and not ahead.

Dalton turned right into an abandoned parking lot behind the dam administration building and came to a stop. There he saw a small, rusting barge in the water straight ahead of them. "That must be it." As the others came into position, he and Rick exited their vehicle, rifles in hand and on the lookout.

5

Déjà Vu

"What do you think? Can they handle being ferried over in the trailer?" Graham asked while the horses, freed from the trailer for now, ate tender green shoots of grass

"It's probably best to leave them in the trailer," McCann answered. "I think they'll be fine. Who's going over first? The barge will only take one truck at a time. Probably should take the horses over last."

"I'd rather not," Graham said. "This place gives me the creeps. We've checked out the buildings, and the doors are locked up tight; it's like they locked down and abandoned the whole facility. Except that someone is keeping it seriously clean. I wonder if those lamps come on at night. It would be awfully dark here without them, or at least the moon, to see by."

"It's a beautiful day," McCann said, taking off his jacket. "Who knew the fog would give way to this? But the problem is, since it's so clear, we can see for miles and so can they—if they're watching, that is."

"I feel a little more comfortable off the road at least. We were sitting ducks out there. We have some cover here for now."

"So, we're boating over to a resort?" McCann asked.

"It's a row of cabins on the water, actually. Ross Lake extends north into Canada. This is Diablo Lake, and at that inlet at the far end"—Graham pointed—"is the river leading to Ross Lake. There's only one road leading to Ross, and it's on the Canadian end, the northern tip; the road goes right up to Hope. So I think we're staying in the cabins on Ross for the night and leaving in the morning," Graham said. "That's the plan, anyway."

McCann looked around their perimeter at the summer homes ringing the lake. "There are a few places here we could stay. How do we know the cabins up there are abandoned?" McCann asked.

Graham looked perplexed, and then a small chuckle escaped him. "That's a good point. It's funny, we find ourselves arrogant in our lone existence now. Sure, there could be people there. Who knows?"

McCann laughed at the thought of their arrogance as he led one of the horses to the lakeshore for a drink. Lifting his hand to shield the sun from his eyes, he said, "We'll find out soon enough, I suppose."

Graham couldn't shake the feeling they were being watched. He held his rifle tightly as he scanned the perimeter past the parking lot. Rick, Reuben, and Dalton were talking near the barge. By the way Rick's hands were moving, Graham figured the men were discussing how to load and run the vehicles into the river and over to Ross Lake from Diablo.

Out of the corner of his eye Graham noticed Bang, who was staring into the woods. His bow and arrow were raised slightly, and there was a perplexed look on his face; Macy held him back by one shoulder, her other hand on the pistol harnessed against her chest. Uneasy about their curious stance, Graham called out as quietly as possible so as not to attract unnecessary attention. "Hey, what's going on over there?"

Macy shot a glance in his direction and then turned back to the scene. "It's Sheriff and the others . . . they've got something, I think." Just then a metallic snap rang out, followed by a dog's painful yelp. Graham knew that snapping metal sound—a trap of some sort. "Get out of there!" he yelled, drawing his weapon and running their way.

As the kids scurried from the woods, Graham and McCann ran toward the yelping. Sheriff appeared through the trees and acted as if he wanted them to follow him; he darted back into the foliage and looked back to see if Graham was behind him.

Ten feet into the woods Graham found Frank, who was yapping in pain and thrashing to free himself of a trap. Sheriff stopped at Frank's side and then looked up at Graham. "I know buddy, I see the trap," Graham said. He knelt down on his good knee, and as McCann came up behind him he shouted, "Grab some sturdy branches! Frank's got himself caught in a bear trap!"

McCann looked down at Frank, whose back leg, caught in the mouth of the rusty contraption, was already matted with blood as red as a Winchester slug shell. While Graham lowered his hand slowly to the dog in a comforting yet cautious gesture, McCann looked around the forest floor for something strong enough to lever open the mouth of the device. Frank howled, but he seemed to know that Graham was there to help him. Sheriff stood by nervously, and Elsa suddenly appeared after having heard Frank's distress.

"Everything okay back there?" Macy called from her position with the others.

Graham didn't want to give any prognosis yet, but McCann responded, "Yeah. Can you call Elsa and Sheriff out of here? Frank got his leg caught in a trap and we need to get it out."

Graham continued to pet and soothe Frank as McCann levered a branch between the jaws of the trap on both sides. As he pried the trap open, Graham pulled the dog's injured limb free. "Aw, damn, that's bad," McCann said.

Frank jumped up, attempting to stand, but let out a yelp, barely putting weight on the leg. "Let's get him back to the others," Graham said. He hefted the dog into his arms while McCann led the way, holding back the brush to help them get through.

In the parking lot Elsa jumped up and tried to sniff at her compadres while McCann fetched his medical supplies. "He's fine," Graham said to reassure Bang, Macy, and Lucy, who were cooing over the dog. "His leg is broken. He'll survive, but he'll probably have a limp for the rest of his life. The rest of you—stay out of the woods. And in the meantime, find some rope and tie up the other dogs!"

Dalton showed up as Graham laid the dog down on the end of the open truck bed for McCann to take over. Brushing dog fur from his shirt Graham said, "Someone is laying traps out; for game, or protection, or both. We're not alone here."

"Yeah, I think you might be right." Dalton looked out across the lake, shielded his eyes from the sun to get a better look past the rippled, reflecting water. "But there's no sign of them on this end other than the traps. I don't think the invaders are responsible for this kind of thing; it's not their style."

"I'm thinking Rick, Sam, and I should go over first and check out the cabins—make sure it's safe and that we're not floating into an ambush. Who knows, there could be survivors over there. It's possible, right? That we're not the last of the infidels? God, I *hope* we're not the last."

Graham made no effort to answer the rhetorical questions. But anything was possible at this point—both good and bad. That was about the only thing Graham was certain of.

6

People, Too

They kept their voices down after that, afraid their words would carry over the wind and water. They quickly huddled and had a bite of their rations, and Dalton relayed the plan to take the first load upriver with Rick and Sam.

"How the hell are we going to get the horse trailer on there?" McCann asked as he watched Rick pilot the small barge loaded down with the first truck, Dalton and Sam keeping guard as the boat lazily floated eastward on the lake.

Reuben shook his head. "Got me. I'd say walk them around, but —he motioned to the mountains around the lake—"I'd say that would take you at least a week."

"Will they keep calm if you walk them onto the barge and just hold them still?" Graham asked.

McCann visualized the situation. Though they had lost one of the horses to the invaders, they still had three altogether. He thought they might come in handy in the future, and leaving them behind would be like abandoning Sheriff. McCann loved the horses, so it just wasn't an option. But having them outside their trailer on a barge in open water, anything could happen—and likely nothing good. He and the horses were guaranteed a long swim in any scenario he could fathom. "No," he said, "they've really got to be in the trailer."

"We're going to have to pull the trailer onto the barge and then load them into it that way," McCann advised. "Operation in reverse when we arrive there. There's not enough room for the trailer and the truck at the same time."

"Graham, do you have leashes for the dogs in case they decide to swim for it?" Reuben asked.

Graham and McCann both looked at Reuben like he was crazy. "A leash? On Sheriff? Heck no," Graham answered. "I don't think we've ever leashed him. It was hard enough getting him tied up just now."

Reuben raised his hands up in a mock-defensive gesture and chuckled. "No offense, but that dog thinks he's people."

Graham nodded, but stared straight ahead. *How do you convey the importance of Sheriff to a man who's never been loved by a dog?* "Sheriff is people. He's one of the finest people I've come across. I'm sure they'll be fine on the water. No leashes necessary."

Graham got along with all the preppers, but at times Reuben rubbed him the wrong way. He wasn't sure what it was, exactly, and this example wasn't one to draw from, but Reuben was a stickler for keeping to the rules of the civilized world—even things like staying within the speed limit or stopping at a stop sign. But in this uncivilized world, such things no longer mattered. Graham had never shared this sentiment with anyone but Tala, as they lay together in the moonlight whispering their innermost thoughts, but something told him McCann felt the same way. The kid kept an eye on Reuben, and a slight distance at all times.

Rick waved at them from the distancing barge, and this broke Graham's train of thought. The sun was high, and there still remained a lot to do before the light was gone, leaving Graham to ponder once again whether the old lamps lining the dam would brighten this vast open space.

7

Cabins on the Lake

"This is a beautiful lake," Rick whispered loudly over the sound of the engine as it pushed the barge through the water. "Don't think I've seen a lake this color before. What's up with that?"

Sam stood aft on the barge, keeping a close eye on the scenery that passed by. "I read a plaque back there. Apparently they call it *mountain flour*. It's from the glaciers grinding away at the moun—"

"Can you guys discuss the unique attributes of our location *after* we arrive safely?" Dalton interrupted from the front of the barge, a firm grip on his rifle and an eye out for any signs of trouble.

"Yes, *sirrr*!" Rick said, giving up on hearing the explanation of why the water was teal blue.

"Hey, look over there!" Dalton yelled. "See that hanger? Let's check that out first."

Rick steered the barge over to where a tan metal hanger sat on the water. When they reached the building, Dalton edged himself over, jumped on the attached dock, and pulled open the hanger door with a loud *clang*. Inside were two seaplanes; they had no use for them right now, so Dalton closed the door, but at least they knew where they were if they ever needed them.

As he climbed aboard the barge again, Dalton felt a moist, refreshing breeze across his face. Rick's long hair blew backward, tickling his ears, and he brushed his arm over his face as he steered the barge to the east end of Diablo and into the Skagit River, which would take them to Ross Lake. The action triggered a memory of Steven; anything slightly humorous always did. It drove Rick crazy when things were quiet like this and he was left with only his thoughts. He rubbed his left hand over his head again, more to brush away the painful memory of his friend.

~

As the river widened into Ross Lake, they could finally see the cabins, just up a bit on the left. Though they were visible from Highway 20, they were still at too great a distance for the invaders to have gotten to them without an advantageous head start. Which reminded Dalton: if there were residents here, it was likely they were watching them at this very moment.

A shiver ran up Dalton's spine. His hand came up, and Rick slowed the barge. Letting the engine idle, Rick looked at Dalton, and then at the cabins. "What do you think?"

Dalton shook his head. "I don't see anything. What do you think, Sam?"

Sam walked up the length of the barge, past the trucks, to Dalton's position and surveyed the area. Several cabins stood in a row with a boardwalk and a dock along the waterfront. He paused. Something wasn't right. Something caused Rick unease too, but he couldn't put his finger on what it was; still, something nagged at him as he looked for any signs of life.

"Too neat," Sam said after a few moments. "Just like the dam area. Someone's cleaning up here." He turned his attention to the tethered boats. "Sure, there are broken limbs and stuff lying around, but these boats would be partially sunk by now with all the storms we've had—not to mention the accumulated snowpack. Someone's been here or *is still* here. Probably set up those traps back on Diablo as a kind of warning too."

"Hello?" Dalton shouted with one hand cupped around his mouth. "Anyone here? We don't want anything from you, and we mean no harm. We're only passing through." The three men watched for any sign or noise that might alert them to the presence of others, but the waves just rippled rhythmically against the side of the barge.

"Move in a little closer, Rick," Dalton said.

The breeze picked up slightly, and Sam slowly raised the business end of his gun. That simple action caused Dalton's heart to race a little bit faster. Sam must have sensed it. "I'm only looking through the scope to get a better look," he said. "Nothing's wrong—yet."

Dalton's vision darted from one side to the other, checking windows for movements, listening for the distinctive click of a shotgun slug chambering action—anything to indicate they were about to be deterred. With his lower lip held firmly in his teeth, they approached the weathered dock and slid alongside a fishing boat.

Rick killed the engine and they stood stock still, crouched and ready for an attack certain to come in the next millisecond. But after nearly a minute, nothing had happened.

Sam broke their vigilance first. "Let's clear it?"

Dalton nodded, motioning with hand signals to Rick to remain on guard. Sam stepped onto the dock and covered their position as Dalton followed him. Dalton couldn't shake the feeling that they were out in the open and a clear open target. He hoped whoever lived here was, at very least, a bad shot. He tapped Sam on the back, and they moved forward together, each watching an end of the boardwalk.

They aimed right at the end of the small dock and went for what appeared to be the office of the establishment. Considering the rooms were probably locked, Dalton thought the keys might be in the office, and instead of wasting time and safety on a probably locked door, they headed straight there. Slow step by slow step, each aiming, each vigilant and acutely aware of what a decrease in their numbers could mean for their overall survival. It came to that, the number of them left; how fleeting lives were, and how easily lost.

"Try the door," said Dalton, breathless, his heart pounding its way out of his rib cage.

Sam grabbed the doorknob and tried to turn it, but it wouldn't budge. He looked at Dalton and shook his head.

Dalton could see that there was no deadbolt located above the doorknob. "Stand back," he said, and as soon as Sam was clear, he raised his boot and quickly sent it to the spot where the lock met the doorframe. The cracking sound of splintered wood sent birds fleeing through the air and crudely reverberated over the tranquil lake like the squeal of tires before an accident.

The white door shot inward, revealing a darkened interior. Dalton braced his back against the doorframe, expecting a volley of bullets to fly toward their position. Even though the temperature was only in the high sixties, sweat covered his face.

"We're not here to hurt you. Don't shoot. Just tell us you're here!" he yelled, further annihilating the peaceful atmosphere. Seconds passed in silence. He nodded toward Sam, took a deep breath, and rushed into the darkened room.

Straining his vision in the dimness, he scanned the room's layout. One door led to the back, another to where the bathroom might be. Sam followed, and they opened each door to check the rooms.

"Clear," Dalton said out of an old habit no longer necessary.

"Are there keys anywhere?"

Breathless from the adrenaline rush, Dalton pointed to a key rack mounted behind the main door.

Sam said, "There's one missing."

"One of the keys?"

"Yeah. Cabin seven."

Dalton looked at the keyboard hanging on the wall and, in fact, keys swung from every hook except the one for cabin 7. "Hmmm . . .

you think there's someone here and they're staying in cabin seven? Can it really be that easy?"

"Maybe someone was left here when the sickness began. Maybe cabin seven is the owner's cabin, or the caretaker's?"

"Well, let's go find out. Grab the keys to the others. We'll clear them along the way. The noise might rattle them out of their hidey-hole."

"There's no doubt in my mind they've heard us by now, if there's anyone here."

Dalton agreed. Whoever was here was either hiding in fear or waiting to ambush them. He had to convince the residents that even though they were trespassing, Dalton's group didn't intend to stay more than one night, and he wanted to warn them about the enemy to the south.

As they exited the office, Rick nodded in their direction. Dalton pointed down to the row of cabins, and Rick understood their intention. Dalton cautiously walked down the row of cabins and Sam followed, covering their rear. An attack could come from any direction, and though they were guarding against the most obvious, they were completely vulnerable.

At cabin 7, the one missing its key, Dalton looked in the window before opening the door. The dark interior showed no signs of life, so he knocked loudly. "Anyone there?" He paused as his plea echoed across the lake. He tilted his head toward the rear of the cabin for Sam to check it out. After a few seconds, Sam called it clear.

Dalton reached for the doorknob and turned it, and the door opened easily. Sam rejoined him, and the two stepped inside. The combination living room and kitchen were clean and neat, with white cabinet fronts and light streaming through a small window framed in cheery yellow plaid curtains above the kitchen sink. The bedroom and loft bunk room slept four easily, and the beds were neatly made. There were no personal items lying about, and no dirty dishes, but there was wood stacked by the woodstove and clean, dry towels hung neatly in the bathroom.

"What's out of place here?" Dalton asked Sam. "Sure, it's a cabin rental, it should be clean and tidy, but what am I missing?"

"It smells fresh," Sam answered. "The upstairs window is cracked open a few inches. Nothing's out of place, and there isn't a musty smell; there would be if that window had been shut the whole time. Someone's keeping this place up." Sam pointed behind Dalton's head toward the door. "There's your missing key." Beside the doorframe, at eye level, key number 7 hung from a hook.

Dalton flipped on a light switch; nothing happened. "No power. Not that I expected it."

"Someone must be maintaining the dam. Leeching out the water after storms, taking care of these cabins. Do you want to keep going, or stay here tonight?"

"As much as I'd like to keep going, it'll take all day to get everyone over here. We'll stay put until tomorrow," Dalton said.

With that they headed back to the boat to drive off the truck. When they were through, Sam stayed with the truck while Rick and Dalton returned with the barge for the next load.

GRAHAM AND MCCANN were left to fend for themselves and the horses as they waited to be picked up for the last trip upriver. The hum of the barge engine faded in the distance as the sun dipped behind the mountains, leaving an atmospheric glow. The breeze off the lake wafted in more of a chill than before. "We're staying in the cabins?" McCann asked, trying to make easy conversation as he held his rifle out, peering into the growing darkness and chewing on a twig.

"Yep. Rotating guard, of course. They say there's no electricity, but there is running water—God help me, I can't figure that one out— and there are clean sheets, on *real* beds. We'll sleep very well, at least for tonight. In shifts, that is."

"Seems kinda creepy if you ask me," McCann said.

Graham chuckled, "Yeah, well, I'll take one night of comfort even if I'm creeped out a bit."

"I'd rather sleep in the woods. Is that weird?"

Graham shook his head, grinning in the dark. McCann was always so serious. They needed that, but Graham was sorry that it was so. McCann never let his guard down, and unfortunately, that's what it took to survive in the world now.

The horses whinnied inside the trailer, and one long tail slapped the side of the gate. Graham happened to be looking at the dam when the lamps suddenly flashed on, saving the dusk from the fading light. "I'll be damned," he said, chuckling at his own wordplay.

"Is it on a battery?"

"I have no idea. We couldn't get inside. The place is locked in a steel casing, like a fort."

"The damn dam . . ." McCann rolled the twig between his teeth.

"Good one." Graham had never heard anything funny come out of McCann, so he encouraged even this simple bit of wordplay.

Suddenly the radio in Graham's hand came to life with Rick's voice. "You guys okay? Over."

"Yeah, we're fine. Over."

"We saw the lights come on. Over."

"Yep. A reminder of the past; someone forgot to turn them off when they left. Over."

"Check. We'll be back in about forty-five. Rick out."

A large crane fly drifted by in the ambient light of the electric torch lamps, and as dusk turned to dark, the soft timbre of the crickets grew louder.

"Nothing they could have done for us anyway, that far away." McCann speculated.

"No, you're right," Graham said. "It's survival, and hope for the best; but if you have to, go down fighting." He flashed suddenly on the wretched image of Dutch's last minutes. *These days, too, shall pass.* He hoped so, for everyone's sake.

GRAHAM TURNED on his flashlight at last when he heard the faint murmur of the barge engine revving louder as it came back across Diablo toward them.

"Finally," McCann said faintly, kicking at the ground with his boot.

Graham knew the young man by now; his anticipation wasn't out of fear as much as distance. McCann never let Macy out of his sight willingly, or for long. Graham understood; his own desire to be beside Tala and protect her grew stronger by the minute.

"Let's get going," McCann said. "Horses out first. Pull the trailer on, then we'll reload them."

In no time they were underway over the lake in the cool early night. Graham guarded the rear of the boat, rifle in hand, as the dam lights faded in the distance; he feared the beacons might be the last artificial light they might ever see, and he wanted the image burned into his memory. He knew that the creation of memories couldn't be a conscious effort, but still he tried.

8

A New Home

"We separated into cabins. I gave you guys one of the larger ones with the extra bedrooms," Clarisse said with a tired smile. The day had been long, and they were all sweaty and tired despite the cool breeze. "The beds are made —with sheets and everything!" she said with wide-eyed surprise.

"Thanks. Which one are we in?" Graham asked, picking up on her enthusiasm.

"Number eight. Same rotation for watch, otherwise, we'll meet up early at the office and get going."

"Perfect. We'll see you guys in the morning, then." Graham waved to Clarisse and Dalton as he and McCann headed off to find cabin 8 at the end of the row along the boardwalk; their footfalls clumping noisily.

The idea of having a shower held almost as much appeal as getting to sleep in a proper bed. Having Tala sleep comfortably for once meant he wouldn't have to worry as much about her or the baby during the night. He was scheduled for watch duty at two in the morning, but that was no problem; he'd pull his four hours and head back to bed and catch a little more sleep before they made their final trek up to Hope.

Ambient light from lanterns, flashlights, and woodstoves gleamed behind the thin curtains of each cabin as they explored their new luxury accommodations for the evening. Tents were an adventure, but having a solid floor under your feet meant security to most. And finally having a little quiet time alone with one's family made this part of the trek a little easier. In the morning, they would again continue to Hope, recharged.

When McCann reached cabin 8, he did the most peculiar thing: he stopped and knocked. "Just open the door," Graham said impatiently

Macy opened the door, smiling at both of them. "Welcome home," she said, waving her arm in a gracious, sweeping gesture to beckon them in.

McCann stood in the doorway, taking it all in; his smile could not have been any wider. Graham clapped him on the back, and they walked into their home, for the night, together. Lamplight softly glowed, filling the space with warmth, and they found Tala standing over a woodstove warming a few cans of beans as Bang fed a few seasoned logs to the fire.

"We'll have a warm dinner tonight, at least. We can't let this wonderful heat go to waste," she said.

Graham slipped his hands around Tala. She'd taken a shower and smelled of soap and shampoo, her hair damp and newly combed. He suddenly realized how much he loved her and that he was really too dirty to be holding her so close to him. "Excuse me. I'll run off to the shower before I eat."

"Yes. Marcy just got out. It's only cold water, but it's wonderful. Soap and shampoo are in there, and there's a change of clean clothes for you too. McCann can go after you. The rest of us have had our turn."

"McCann, keep watch out front," Graham said.

"Sure, no problem."

"The watch rotation is on," Marcy said. "You can relax."

Mark shook his head. "We're *always* on watch, Marcy."

"Where's Sheriff?" Graham asked.

"He's outside," Macy said. "I'll let him back in when he shows up. The other two stayed with Lucy. She's bunking with Clarisse and Dalton, and Clarisse is tending to Frank."

"That makes me feel better. I'm glad Lucy isn't alone and having to deal with Frank's injury on her own." Tala said. "And how is Frank, anyway? Poor dog."

"Clarisse set his broken leg and made a splint for him; she said he'd heal in time."

As Graham entered the bathroom, it hit him that it was the first time he'd found himself completely alone in the past several days. Having his own group—his family—alone and under one roof made him feel more secure, but the uncertainty of what awaited them in the coming days lingered.

In the bathroom, Tala had placed a one-gallon bottle of water and secured an elastic headlamp around the base. The effect was a soft ambient glow that radiated through the water; just enough to see by. She didn't trust the kids to have an oil lamp in the bathroom; too many accidents were possible. The woman was resourceful, he'd give her that. She was always coming up with smart solutions to everyday problems.

Graham ran his hands through his oily hair and over his beard and then began to scratch his neck. "You are one dirty somebitch," he said to his reflection in Ennis's voice. He still missed the man.

Stop it. Don't go there.

Then, he eyed the shower. In doubt he turned the knob, and to his surprise, water began to trickle out.

I'll be damned. Still can't figure this one out.

In no time he was clean. Cold from the frigid water, but clean and dressed in fresh clothes. To live this life made you appreciate the simple things—clean clothes and bathing being high on that list. He flipped off the light after he emerged from the bathroom, and then McCann eagerly took his turn.

The smell of baked beans wafted throughout the cabin. "Man that smells so good," Graham said to the group sitting in the front room.

"Tala found an unopened bottle of barbecue sauce in the kitchen cupboard," Bang said, his eyes wide and excited.

Graham raised his eyebrows. "So, barbecue beans? Even better." He sat down on the beige couch between the twins, who were silently zoning out at the fire within the woodstove. Mark halfheartedly stood guard at the window, watching the moon's reflection on the rippled lake. Tala sat in a comfortable living room chair, and Bang was on the floor in front of her. Graham let out a loud sigh. The fire crackled and occasionally popped, and everyone sat in contemplation without speaking or even looking at one another, drifting into the safety of silence and appreciating these creature comforts.

Tala finally looked up at Graham, breaking his trance. When their eyes met, she asked, "Hungry?"

He chuckled. "When am I *not*?"

Macy yawned loud and long. Mark, still staring out the window, reached for the door handle.

"What's up?" Graham asked him.

"Sheriff. He's wandering around, looking for us out there." He opened the door and whistled low. Sheriff ran to the door, and in no time he'd settled down on the floor next to Bang, licking him in the radiant heat of the woodstove. He sniffed and then eyed the pot on the woodstove like Tala knew he would, and she said right off, "No."

Sheriff averted his eyes from Tala but licked his chops.

"It's okay, Sheriff. I've got something for you," said Macy. "I found a few cans of actual dog food under the sink in the kitchen. I'll give one to him now, and save the other two for Frank and Elsa." She got up and called Sheriff into the kitchen as Bang followed her.

Soon all could hear the unmistakable sound of Sheriff enjoying an unusually hearty meal; Bang and Macy giggled at the sight of it. Soon they heard the water from McCann's shower stop, and Tala stirred the beans in the pot while Marcy located several bowls and spoons; moments later they passed around heaping bowls of barbecue beans with a surprise side of saltine crackers.

"Look what else we found," Macy said.

"Monopoly?" McCann said.

"Yeah. Let's play!" she said.

"I'll keep watch at the door. You guys go ahead and play," Graham said.

He couldn't get over this serene moment. They'd been through hell in the last several days. Scenes of it reran through his mind, torturing him day and night, and yet here they were, enjoying an evening in solace, having escaped with their lives. They were vigilant, of course, but so precarious was their position, so subject were they to death's will. So close—and yet, they were alive.

With bowls full of beans and crackers, they settled the Monopoly game on the living room floor. Graham glanced at them between shoveling food into his mouth and keeping watch outside. They giggled and laughed, and soon Tala was yawning. It was contagious, and everyone else began to do the same. They never finished the game, but decided it was a tie and that Mark cheated; he was the designated banker, and they were convinced he'd slipped himself a few extra hundred. They wrapped it up, and the girls said, "goodnight," and headed upstairs to a bedroom with Sheriff close behind. Bang and Mark were sleeping in the opposite room upstairs, and McCann had the couch in the living room. Graham and Tala cleaned up the dishes and then wandered into their own room, clean sheets and all.

9

A Surprise

Graham tried to be quiet as he snuck out of the bedroom at two o'clock. Tala slept so peacefully he didn't want to wake her, yet the door creaked as he pulled it open.

"Graham?" Tala murmured.

"It's okay. Go back to sleep. I've got watch duty," he said. She rolled over and pulled the covers up to her shoulders. Graham closed the door and stepped out into the living room, put his boots on, and headed for the door as McCann snored loudly on the couch. He put his hand on the doorknob and suddenly McCann was upright with his rifle aimed at the front door—and Graham by extension. His eyes were glazed over, his sleep-tousled hair was a wild nest, and he had the look of a pissed-off and armed madman.

Graham's hands shot into the air. "McCann! It's just me! I'm on watch. See you later." McCann fell back into the couch. Two things came to Graham's mind: *Do not screw with McCann in sleep mode, and thank God he's a hostile sleeper.*

Once out in the night, Graham wasn't surprised to see his own breath in the wind. It was cold; the night's low must have hit freezing. He quietly walked up the boardwalk to the dock, where Rick was stationed by the barge.

"Mornin'," Graham said, nodding.

"Not for me . . . yet," Rick said, wiping his tired eyes.

"Anything to report?" Graham asked while Rick handed him the radio and night vision goggles.

"No, not really. There was some shuffling in the woods earlier, but I figured it was deer. It's hard to hear well over the rippling water, and sounds travel differently on a lake. I tried not to walk around too much on the pier to keep the noise level down so everyone could sleep. Keep watch on the highway as much as you can"—he pointed across the lake—"but I didn't see a thing. Watch out for the moonlight's reflection with the goggles, they blind you if you hit it just right. Sam is taking over for Clarisse right now at the back of the cabins; I just saw her head in. That's it, I think. I'm toast. Good night."

"'Night Rick. Sleep well."

"I plan to," he said, yawning as he headed back down the pier to his own temporary sanctuary and softly sheeted bed.

Graham raised the NVGs and checked the perimeter from his current position. He had two hours of watch, and somehow he doubted he'd get back to sleep.

They were pretty isolated here, with steep mountains on all sides. Farther up, at the north end of the lake, a lone road would lead the way out of the United States. In the morning they would begin the process again, loading the vehicles one by one onto the barge and heading up the lake to that road. Then, hopefully, by tomorrow night they might find another place to sleep—or "tent it," as Dalton would say.

The lake ripples splashing against the pillars of the dock seemed a hypnotic cadence, and Graham decided it was time for a walk. He kept his steps light and began traversing the boardwalk, heading first one way and then the other. Midway, he caught a glimpse of Sam's headlamp at the back through the breezeway of the cabins. Graham nodded his own headlamp in salute, Sam nodded back, and the two of them resumed their watch.

It wasn't until the solitude erupted into utter chaos that they talked again. One minute Graham was lost in thought, and the next thing he knew, all of the lights within each cabin, in every room, flashed on. Every cabin radio switched on to blare static noise at its highest volume, there was a cacophony of dogs barking, and everyone began spilling out of the cabins frightened, armed, and confused.

"What the hell is going on?" Rick yelled after it was clear no bullets were flying.

"It's got to be a diversion," Sam yelled back. "Let's get everyone back in the cabins!"

"Go back inside, and turn everything off!" Graham yelled over the chaos. He glanced over to cabin 8 and saw his crew standing outside with Sheriff in the lead; McCann poised to shoot anything that moved.

Then Dalton, dressed only in his jeans but carrying his M14, began ushering folks inside to flip switches off. Moments later everything was silent again. Several watched from their windows, too jarred to go back to sleep.

"What do you think that was?" Rick asked as they huddled near the pier.

"Heck if I know," Sam said, "it sure as hell wasn't the jihadists. They prefer bullets over annoyance attacks."

Graham's heart still beat from the sudden rush of adrenaline. "It's got to be that dam guy."

"What damn guy?" Rick asked confused.

"Whoever's at the dam, keeping things so clean; that's no accident of caretaking. Someone is there keeping the spillway in check, cleaning up and maintaining things. Maybe there are generators or turbines still left from Ross Dam, and he's linked electricity to the cabins from them. That would also explain why we have running water—the water pump must be on a separate circuit." He shook his head. "Dammit, he's probably inside that steel dam building, and he probably watched us."

After a second of silence, Rick said, "You sound a little bit paranoid, Graham."

Dalton suppressed a chuckle.

"Look, I ran into a guy like that not too long ago, outside Seattle, where Bang, the girls, and I came from. He was the self-appointed *mayor* of the town, a real nutcase. I'm telling you, it's not a good sign, and I don't think we should hang around here. We should leave —*now*."

"It's still too dark," Dalton said. "Let's give it a few more hours."

"No one's going to go back to sleep now anyway," Graham said, pointing to the cabin directly in front of them. "He's warning us. I don't want to be here to see what happens next."

Dalton turned and saw Lucy and Addy's frightened faces peering out the window of his own cabin. He shook his head in frustration.

"He could have rigged the juice to generators," Rick added. "It's plausible; I'm with Graham. Fool me once, shame on you; fool me twice, shame on me. I'm going to fall asleep, and that crap is going to happen all over again. He booby-trapped this place, leaving all the switches on. Screw it. Let's pack up and get the hell out of here."

Dalton held up his hands. All right. We're all awake, whether we like it or not." He stared out toward a faint glow in the sky that had to be coming from the dam lights. "Maybe it was his way of telling us to get out. Let's go ahead and begin packing things up."

10

On the Border

In time everyone's belongings were packed. The first vehicle, including Sam, was already across the border and waiting in Canada, but this would be an all-day undertaking.

"I think I should leave a few doses of the vaccine for the dam guy," Clarisse said.

Dalton stood on the boat dock waiting for Rick to make his way back. He could see him in the distance and barely heard the hum of the engine as it approached. "Uh-uh, no way," Dalton said. "He scared the crap out of us and turned the lights on. No, the dam guy can do without."

They were having a little fun with the name.

"He's just a crazy dam guy. What if he gets exposed to us and dies?"

"Screw the dam guy. How do we know there's just one? Hell, it might be a dam girl. You're sexist." Dalton smiled at Clarisse.

"Seriously, you're infuriating. I should leave a few vials with a thank-you note. We might have to come back this way again someday."

"Think about what you're saying. Would you inject yourself with something left by strangers claiming it would cure you of the incurable?"

Clarisse pondered the situation. "That's a good point. Screw the dam guy," she began to walk away. "I have several left. I'll pack them in a cooler and leave them in the office anyway. Can't hurt," she said, and he shook his head at her insistence.

When Rick approached, Dalton noticed he looked awful—pale and drawn. "As soon as we get underway, you're sleeping. That's an order. Why don't we have Reuben pilot the barge for a while?"

"No, I can do it. This place is starting to give me the creeps. Let's get the hell out of here as soon as possible."

"Okay. Next up is Reuben's truck. We're all pretty much ready to go."

By the time they were finished loading the truck onto the barge, the sunrise was beginning to bloom. The birds began chirping as Rick finished a cup of coffee someone had pushed into his hand.

AFTER THE THREE more trips and many hours, the only thing left was the horse trailer. Dalton stayed on with McCann, awaiting the barge's return. He checked out the office and found that Clarisse had, in fact, left a note and three vials of the vaccine on ice in a spare cooler with instructions. He thought it strange, but perhaps the dam guy hadn't meant to scare them after all. Maybe he only wanted to make contact in the only way he knew how. It didn't matter now. They were leaving, and if the dam guy was watching, he would see that they'd left him a present. When they came back—and they *would* come back—they'd find out for sure who this dam guy was.

Dalton secured the lid on the cooler so the vaccine would stay viable for several days under those conditions. He hoped it wouldn't go to waste. He closed the front door of the office and in the bright afternoon sun that still carried a nip in the spring air, he walked back to McCann's station next to the horse trailer as the barge floated up to the dock.

THE ROAD they were to take started at the north end of Lake Ross and led farther north, away from the border. It would be the last they'd see of the United States until they came up with a plan to return and take it back. Dalton stood on the back of the barge as they crossed the border. It killed him to leave his own country, and he vowed they'd be back. He wouldn't let the jihadists just have it, but for now, he reluctantly said good-bye, with one consolation: America was in the hearts of those who traveled with him, and together they would fight for their home no matter what it took.

11

Sleep Talker

They were driving on pavement once again, and Rick settled down in the backseat of Sam's truck. He didn't care where he was, really, as long as he could shut his eyes and get some sleep. He was the only one who hadn't had a chance to shower in an actual shower or sleep in an actual bed, but he didn't care; the farther he got his wife and daughter away from the terrorists the better. In a few hours, they would be near Hope. He would be rested, and they could begin to make plans to rid themselves of those animals once and for all.

He had a few ideas, but they came during dreams, and though he tried to grasp them, he wasn't sure if they were real or if his mind was simply trying to allay his fears during sleep. In any event, he thought of little else, and a few tricks were beginning to take form. He had no concrete plan as of yet, but he was working on one.

"Rick!" Sam yelled. The voice sounded far off. "Rick!" Sam yelled again.

What the hell does he want?

"*Rick!*"

"What?" Rick yelled back.

"Time to wake up. We're almost there, but we're stopping for a bit. Dalton wants to regroup before we get too close to Hope in case we meet up with anyone there."

"I've been asleep *all day?*"

"Yeah. You've been talking in your sleep, too. Snoring like a damn bazooka," Sam said gruffly, looking genuinely annoyed.

Rick rubbed his head. "I feel like we just left."

Sam got out of the truck with haste and grabbed his rifle. "That was hours ago, and I've been a prisoner to your noise long enough."

"Sam?" Rick called out, but he'd already slammed the truck door shut.

What the heck was I talking about?

Rick climbed out of the truck and found Sam talking to Olivia beside the road, where she'd set up a coffee dispenser for those who wanted a caffeine jolt; at the same time, Lucy handed out meal packets and water bottles for dinner.

"No, he's riding with you the rest of the way," Rick could hear Sam say as he approached.

"Olivia was kind enough to marry you," Sam said. "You can ride with her the rest of the way." He walked off, coffee in hand.

"What is his problem?" Rick asked as Olivia handed him a cup.

"Your snoring could drive any sane man crazy, Rick. Why do you think I sleep with earplugs?"

Before he could retort, Dalton interrupted. "Okay, everyone, listen up. The sun will be setting soon, and I think we have another half hour before we enter Hope. It's the largest town we've been to since . . . well, since the bear attack. Anyway, it's geographically secluded, but there may be people there. We just don't know anything yet. Remember, there may still be individuals out there who are susceptible to the pandemic, so keep your distance. And let's all stick together; don't get separated. Any questions?"

"Where are we going to stop?" Tala asked.

"We have a map, but none of us has actually been there before. So we'll head into town and stop at the first accessible place we can bunk for the night. Tomorrow we'll check things out and see what's available. We'll look at a school or a larger building we can use for the night.

"This is dangerous. We don't know what's out there, but it's our chance to survive for a while away from the terrorists who've taken over our country. Be vigilant, and stay together."

They dispersed to their vehicles, Rick riding with Olivia and the children. As usual, Dalton led the caravan and Reuben brought up the rear.

The western sky turned a flamboyant cast of purple at dusk as they headed north through the last winding curves of the two-lane road leading to Hope. Because the road was flanked by evergreen trees, it might as well been the middle of the night; visibility was low, and having to maneuver the caravan around several fallen trees took time and patience.

The drive reminded Graham of when he, the twins, Bang, and Sheriff first drove into Cascade. It seemed like only yesterday. He remembered thinking at one point then that everything was just a dream until he looked to the passenger seat and saw a sleepy little six-year-old or in the rearview mirror to glance at the twins and the police dog in the back. Then he would remember why they were there together—it was no dream—and his vision would shift to the world outside the car's window.

"Are we there yet?" came Bang's voice from the backseat.

Tala looked at Graham and stifled a laugh.

What a normal thing for a child to say.

"We'll be there soon, buddy. You okay?" Graham asked.

"Yeah," he said.

"If you get tired, Bang, just go ahead and sleep," Tala said.

Since the last stop, both Bang and Sheriff had opted to ride with Graham, and he could tell the boy had had enough of the long trip. After a while, he could see neither Bang nor Sheriff in the darkened back seat of the Scout and assumed they had gone to sleep.

They traveled in silence, Graham and Tala both deep in thought. After a few more winding curves, the brake lights of Dalton's truck shone bright in front of them, and Graham noticed a building on the left up ahead.

"Guess this is it?" Tala said.

"Might be."

Graham put the truck into park and watched as Dalton exited the driver's side and walked back to the Scout. Graham wasn't sure why he didn't just use the radio. *Maybe he needs to walk a little.*

Graham rolled down his window and allowed the cool evening air to spill inside. Tala pulled a blanket around herself.

"What's up?"

"We're on the edge of town. There's a roadblock ahead," Dalton said.

"Hmmm—past or present?" Graham asked.

"Looks pretty current. There's a light. I didn't want to use the radio in case there's an intercept. We don't know who we're dealing with here."

"Doesn't sound like the invaders' standard operating procedure to put up a light at a roadblock."

"No, it doesn't; looks more military. There might be more people here than we thought," Dalton speculated.

"What do you want to do?" Graham asked.

"I think . . . Rick and I should approach on foot. See if anyone comes to greet us."

"Like the Welcome Wagon?" Graham kidded.

"Yeah, why not? It could happen. We're due for a break, after all." Rick and Sam now approached after climbing out of their own vehicles.

Graham listened as Dalton relayed the plan, and pretty soon everyone shut off their vehicles to conserve fuel. Both Rick and Dalton geared up with heavier coats and larger weapons. They both wore NVGs loosely around their necks, since night had blackened their world completely in the little time it took them to get ready.

Graham waved at them as they passed his truck and watched as

Dalton stopped at the lead truck and spoke to Clarisse. It was the first time he'd seen them kiss in public. Clarisse's shadow climbed over the driver's seat as he reached for her in the cab. It was an intimate moment, and Graham found himself looking away and then at Tala in the dark. He found her knee and held it tight. She covered his hand with her own. There were times in life that nothing need be said, and this was one of those moments.

Dalton gave the signal to turn off the headlights of the parked vehicles, and almost in unison they did so, plunging them all into total darkness. They were on their way. Sam was on watch somewhere, and everyone was on order to stay off the radios.

Graham assumed that Dalton and Rick would be gone a few minutes and then find a way to get around an abandoned roadblock.

But that's not what happened. Not by a long shot.

12

Hospitality

S am stood at the tree line, watching carefully through his NVG goggles as Rick and Dalton walked toward the roadblock. Reuben was guarding the rear of the convoy. Before the two had set off, Sam had warned them that the roadblock looked active, and something about the setting bothered him, but both Rick and Dalton seemed unconcerned.

They're getting lax and tired. Something bad's going to happen. I can just feel it. No sooner had the thought crossed Sam's mind than he found himself reeling from bright lights that pierced his pupils. It was a shocking transition; the NVGs, intended for use in the dark, blinded those who were exposed to sudden flashes of light.

"Oh my God!" he yelled, pulling off the goggles and rubbing his eyes. Suddenly someone shoved him to the ground hard from behind, and Sam heard the zipping sound of PlastiCuffs binding his wrists. He was a prisoner before he even had a chance to think.

Sam began blindly kicking at whoever had attacked him when he heard the distinct crying of his daughter Addy among a cacophony of screams. He stopped stone cold as his watery vision recovered. Armed men in Tyvek suits were pulling everyone out of their vehicles and lining them up against the trucks.

"She can't hear!" Clarisse screamed at one suited man who had a hysterical Addy by the arm as she tried to flee to her father. "Please let me take her."

Thank God, Sam thought. He rolled over to see who had accosted him just in time to catch the butt end of a rifle slamming into the side of his head.

Moments later he came to, and found himself in the back of an enclosed truck, with Graham stemming the flow of blood coming from the wound in his head.

"What the hell happened?"

Graham shook his head quickly as an indication to Sam to keep silent. Sam shifted his eyes over to two suited guys sitting at the back of the truck, guns pointed in their direction.

"Not very humorous, are they," Sam mumbled.

"One more word out of you and he dies," one of the guards said. His rifle was aimed at McCann, who was seated in front of them with more than one bleeding wound to the head. Sam took one look at McCann and figured the young man had probably tried to fight his way through but had come out at the wrong end.

Sam nodded, looking up at Graham again. Graham tugged him into a sitting position, which he greatly appreciated since the pressure of his weight on his arms was causing them to go numb. He could now see that the truck contained all the men from their group, including Rick and Dalton, and all were handcuffed except for Graham.

"Keep your hands where we can see them," the guard yelled, and Graham immediately held them up. "He's fine now, sit up there and keep your hands where we can see them."

Sam wanted more than anything to know where Addy was, but as he looked around at everyone it was clear they weren't speaking for a reason. Now and then one of them would make eye contact with him and then look down or off into their world, but no one tried even as much as a nod or to communicate in any way. He decided to follow their lead, since he didn't understand the precarious position they now found themselves in.

He knew two things: they were traveling somewhere, given the vibration of the vehicle, and the voices of the two guards sounded more Canadian than anything foreign, so he'd bet they were not the Islamic terrorists. He couldn't help thinking that he had known something wasn't right at the roadblock and he'd botched communicating that to Dalton.

EVERYONE LOOKED up at the guards expectantly and each other when the truck slowed with a squeak of the brakes before coming to a final stop. The guards rose and waited at the door. There were two pounds against the outside of the truck, and the guards responded with two more. The door swung open, and they stepped out. There six other men were also dressed in Tyvek and armed to the hilt, pointing their weapons at the inside of the vehicle.

"You"—the guard pointed to Graham—"step down here and help them off one by one. We're going this way." He pointed toward a dark gate, behind which was a doorway with minimal light. "Do anything stupid and all the women and children will be exterminated immediately along with the rest of you. No talking; no communicating. We don't want any accidents. Any sudden moves, someone will die. Let's go."

Sam glanced at Dalton, who looked back at him with a stone straight face. Nothing to lead him to think they should act. These guys were obviously still susceptible to the virus. They outnumbered —and by the looks of things, out armed—Graham and the preppers' group. They had no options, and Sam had no idea how these men had managed to overtake them so easily.

Rick rose first after Graham, as the guard said, and stood by the back of the truck. Everyone else had their hands wrapped securely behind their backs with the plastic cuffs. Sam's guess is that they didn't find Graham that much of a threat with his limp: he wouldn't get far out of shooting range if he ran.

Sam got in line behind Reuben, and once the rest were off, Graham was allowed to help McCann up off the bench. It was the first time he'd noticed that McCann not only had his hands tied behind his back but his legs were also tied at the ankles and his knees were even cuffed together.

Sam had to stifle a snicker as he watched the young man hobble forward, not at McCann's predicament but at the thought of how he must have given them hell.

One of the guards held up his rifle and said, "One false move and that's it, kid. I'm not putting up with your bullshit. You understand?" McCann nodded, and another guard walked over with wire cutters and pinched off the PlastiCuffs holding his legs and feet together.

Graham helped McCann climb down and guided him as they headed toward the dim gate.

"Keep walking," the guard demanded, holding open a brown steel door. As they were ushered into a brick building, Sam caught a glimpse of the outside. There were steel bars over the windows and a heavy industrial lock on the door; an unmistakable feeling of finality jolted him as the door slammed shut behind them and they were left in a dimly lit room.

13

A Greeting

"I'm Lieutenant Harding. Who are you, and what are you doing here?" Clarisse sat on the metal chair inside a quarantine room as he questioned her through glass.

It had been a while since they'd seen anyone alive—too long—and before he'd begun any questioning he had observed her. She had been checking out the room with an educated eye; this woman was trained, and that made her dangerous. He couldn't take any chances.

Clarisse's eyes again darted around the room. She noted his sidearm, the laboratory behind him, and the microscopes on the table, though she squinted a great deal as she tried to gain focus.

Her dark hair had come loose during the struggle, and she kept attempting to get it out of her eyes, but with her hands in restraints behind her, Clarisse found the task difficult.

Harding rather liked the way her hair spilled down over her shoulders; otherwise, he might have given her a chance to fix it. Still, the offer would be too risky; this woman had fought with tenacious skill. Whoever these people were, they were here for a reason, and he needed to find out what it was—and fast. Something told him his own people were in danger, and he'd spent a lot of time and effort protecting them; one slip now and they could lose everything. As it was, the pretty woman opposite the glass could kill him with one breath.

"You're not going to answer me, are you."

Clarisse locked eyes with him, adding a slight smile.

Damn, she's dangerous. Christ! He coughed.

She leaned back and crossed her legs. "Where are the men?" she asked.

Startled by her sweet-sounding voice, Harding glanced at her in surprise. He'd expected her voice to be more direct, even harsh. "They're safe. But their remaining so depends on you." He tapped the eraser end of his pencil on the table.

"I've got something you want."

He coughed again and tapped the eraser faster against the paper pad. *You sure do*, he thought, but caught himself, instead saying, "I don't think you're in a position to negotiate, lady." He swung his pencil in a radius around the room. He smiled a little, but she hadn't cracked; not a twitch or even an eyelash out of place, just the same steely gaze. *Damn, she knows something I don't.*

"Where did you come from? We tracked you coming in." She still hadn't moved. He leaned back, feigning a relaxed posture, and turned at an angle in his chair. She was making him nervous. "Look, give me some information, and then we can talk," he almost begged. *Sheesh, who's interrogating who here?* Moments passed in silence, and she still had that damn smile. But suddenly Clarisse stood up and walked to the door, her metal chair screeching along the concrete flooring.

"What? We're done?" Harding rose from his own chair, causing it to screech backward. *This woman has some balls.* Clarisse stood at the exit door and without looking at him or acknowledging his existence, just waiting.

The guard looked at Harding through the glass for some direction. He shook his head. "Go ahead; take her back." Turning to

Clarisse, he said, "When you're ready to talk, tell the guard. Otherwise, enjoy your confinement."

She was out the door before he finished the sentence. He gathered up the papers strewn over the table when someone knocked on the door. "Come in," he said gruffly.

"Hey Harding, Gordon wants to see you," the guard said.

"Of course he does." Harding dropped his pencil on top of the papers he had just assembled into a tidy stack. They'd taken in people before, not long after the lockdown; they'd been tested and cleared, assimilated and trained. But this was different. These folks were immune somehow. Carriers, most likely, and dangerous as hell. It was the agreed-upon policy to exterminate them because they posed an incredible risk to society at large, and Harding knew Gordon would push for immediate disposal. It wasn't that simple, though; these were people. Was it humane to gas them? That was the plan. He pondered how to bargain for more time; he needed to know what was going on out there. *"I've got something you want," she'd said.* Harding hoped to hell she broke soon, because he wasn't sure how long he could hold Gordon off from pressing the button. *Christ, they have a pregnant woman with them too.* He picked up his pile of papers and headed for the door, looking back through the safety glass at the steel chair where the woman had sat. He looked behind his seat at what she was trying to focus on earlier, and then had an idea. He let the heavy door slam shut as he exited.

14

The Prisoners

Clarisse walked through the door as the guard halted her from behind. He snipped the PlastiCuffs free from her wrists and then nudged her forward before slamming the door shut again.

Addy ran to her side. "Clarry!" she said in a broken, scared voice.

"I'm fine," she signed, and then pressed the girl to her side in a warm embrace. Tala approached next. "What did they want?"

"They don't know what they're doing," she whispered. "But remember, this place could be bugged. Have they brought any rations?"

Tala shook her head.

"They just want to know who we are and what we're doing here. They told me more about them in the past hour than I'll ever tell them. They're susceptible. They're military. And they're clueless. Which makes them dangerous to themselves and to us," she confided.

"Are the guys okay?"

"I think so, but I don't know for sure," she said.

"What are we going to do?"

"We have water from the bathroom faucet. If they don't bring rations by tomorrow, I'll raise hell. How's Macy doing?"

Tala looked across the dimly lit room to the cot where they'd placed an unconscious Macy upon arrival. "She hasn't woken up yet, but her breathing's fine."

Clarisse shook her head. "Thank God. We could have easily lost her and McCann both in that struggle. Soon as I get my hands on that boy I'm going to strangle him—after I hug him, that is."

"She saved his life. They almost made it into the woods. Had she not jumped in between him and the guard, he'd be dead for sure."

"I was too far forward. I didn't see what happened. I only heard the gunshot after the struggle," Clarisse said.

"Well, McCann had Macy out of the truck and they were headed for the woods when the guards confronted them. McCann, of course, wasn't going to comply and instead attacked the guards. Then Macy got in between them and then, well, the gunshot went off after Sheriff came to Macy's aid."

"Oh my God. Where's Sheriff? Was he shot?"

Tala was crying then. She pulled her hands up to her mouth to keep from sobbing and shook her head. "I don't know. I couldn't see that far in the dark."

"It's going to be okay," Clarisse said, hugging her friend.

"What am I going to tell Macy when she wakes up?" Tala whispered. "It'll kill her!"

Clarisse pulled herself away. "Look. We're lucky *she* wasn't shot. She just has a concussion, as far as I can tell. As for Sheriff, maybe she already knows. She was the only real witness besides McCann." She paused. "Maybe the guard missed, or it was intended as an attention-getter, a warning. We can't worry about Sheriff right now."

"Where are the other dogs?" Tala asked

"Lucy said the guard told her to leave them in the cab as she got out, but they ran off after the commotion."

"They're still out there?"

"I don't know." Clarisse shrugged. "I'm sure by now these buffoons are searching through every vehicle we came in. I hope to hell they don't screw with my equipment. Then again, our release depends on what they find within my research cache."

"Hope," Tala said. "Not exactly what we were hoping for."

"Don't worry. I think I know what's going on here. I think we'll be free within a week."

15

Interrogation

"I'll bet you my coffee rations that they come for Graham first," Rick speculated.

"What makes you think they'll pick me?" Graham asked.

"You're the most reasonable looking," Dalton answered.

"You mean *educated*," Graham said with slight smile.

"You're the nerd. The unthreatening nerd," Rick clarified.

Graham chuckled and leaned back against the cold brick wall.

"You don't *have* any coffee rations," Dalton said after a minute.

"You know, when I get some. I bet my *future* coffee rations that Graham will be the first one questioned," Rick said.

"I don't think they're going to question any of us. My bet is that they're questioning Clarisse right about now," Dalton said. "They'd damn well better not hurt her."

Graham laughed out loud,

"What?" Dalton asked, looking at Graham like he was crazy.

"Are we talking about the same Clarisse I was with in our attempt to rescue Dutch? Those guys have bought a world of trouble on themselves if they think they'll get anything out of her. She'll tear every one of them a new one."

Dalton smiled. "Yeah, this is true. She knows what she's doing." He leaned his head back against the wall and closed his eyes. "Whoever they come and get for questioning, be very careful. Remember, you're putting the women in danger. If anything happens to them, you'll be dealing with me—if you survive." He opened his eyes, and the other guys looked lost in thought. It didn't need saying. Dalton was just scared, and they all knew that.

"At least we know they loaded the kids with the ladies into the other truck together. That's a good sign," Rick said, trying to change the subject.

"Yeah. Bang's probably scheming an escape route as we speak. They have no idea who they're dealing with," Graham said.

"Someone's coming," Mark said from his position by the door.

The men looked to one another for direction. Each had his area of expertise, yet no exact initiative had ever been taken regarding who would handle imprisonments.

"Everyone stay calm," Dalton said. "And McCann—no heroics."

McCann nodded from his pallet on the floor but looked at Sam, who nodded back in understanding.

The lock threw back loudly, and the heavy door swung open. Bright light streamed in, causing the men to cover their eyes momentarily. A dark figure stepped inside, flanked by two other suited individuals. "Who's in charge here?"

When no one answered, one of the guards kicked Mark's leg. "You. Who gives the orders in this group?"

Mark instinctively looked to Dalton and Graham, making no difference between the two.

"All right, it's one of those two," the guard said. "You two, get up."

Neither Graham nor Dalton moved.

"I said, *get up!*" the guard ordered, chambering a round, and this caused McCann to rise from his pallet, the veins bulging in his neck. Graham couldn't take it anymore; he knew the boy would react if challenged, so he pushed himself up from the floor. Dalton followed.

"Where are we going?" Dalton asked.

"To see Lieutenant Harding. He's requested a meeting with you," the guard said. He waved his hand around the room. "Take a look around you. Try anything, and they die, one by one. You understand? You shouldn't even be here. If it were my choice, I'd have done away with you by now."

As they left the room, Graham shot McCann a look that pleaded for calm.

THEIR HANDS WERE CUFFED behind their backs again, and the bright light of the afternoon blinded them as they were led to another brick building. Graham tried to make out where they were, but the unmarked buildings gave him no clues. They could be at an abandoned school or an old military installation—or perhaps even a cheese factory for all he knew. He did, however, spot one of their trucks parked nearby.

"Hey, keep up," the guard behind him yelled as he nearly stepped on the back of Graham's boot.

"If you guys are susceptible to the virus, you should keep your distance, be more careful," Graham shot back.

"Are you threatening me?" the guard yelled.

Everyone stopped.

Graham turned around to look at the guard, and his face turned serious but unthreatening. "No. I'm not. But I mean it; please keep your distance. I really don't want you to get the virus."

"He's being honest, man," Dalton interjected. "You shouldn't be so close that you're running into us. Those suits can only protect you so far." He took a step toward the guard. "You guys have been isolated here the whole time, haven't you?"

Graham and Dalton made eye contact, and the guards took two large steps backward.

The lead guard said, "That's enough. Just keep walking."

These guys have no idea what they're dealing with, Graham thought. Soon they entered another building, and when the guards held the door open they both kept a greater distance.

Two chairs faced a glass window; behind it, a man in military uniform sat in what reminded Graham of Clarisse's lab back in Cascade.

"Have a seat, gentlemen," the man said, gesturing through the glass toward the seating arrangement. Graham had no idea how to handle a situation like this, but Dalton had told him earlier that if they were questioned to give up no information. None whatsoever.

The man behind the glass made no eye contact as he began scribbling notes with a pencil on a few papers strewn across a lab counter, acting as if Dalton and Graham's presence was a hindrance to his already overburdened schedule after the apocalypse. Graham wasn't sure what to think, but he guessed the man's behavior was probably some kind of ploy, and from Dalton's half smile he knew his friend was already in the lead.

The man finally sat up, tearing his attention away from his notes but acting surprised they were still sitting there. Dalton relaxed his posture, practically melting into the chair, and Graham followed suit.

"I'm Lieutenant Harding. And you are—?" The man poised his pencil to write their answer, but neither of them said a thing.

He looked back up at them. "Really? Games?" He let out a frustrated huff. "Look, I just had one of your ladies in here and she spilled it. You might as well come clean. We've searched your convoy. We know you're American refugees. We know you're contagious. Tell me why we should keep you alive. Give me some reason not to exterminate all thirty of you."

After nearly a full minute of silence, Graham wanted Dalton to speak. They were reasonable questions, but he trusted Dalton's experience; there had to be a reason he wasn't offering any information.

The guy looked from Graham to Dalton and then began tapping the pencil's eraser against the desk. Dalton never flinched.

"You have a pregnant woman with you," he said, shaking his

head. "She looks to be about eight months along. You came to Hope for a reason. Are you trying to escape from something? Is the United States exterminating the carriers?"

Graham watched the man's expression and thought he was genuinely guessing, pleading with them for some kind of answer, and this caused Dalton to deduce that these Canadians had no idea about the terrorists. And if they had no idea about the terrorists, they were extremely naive and vulnerable, which also meant they were all, Americans and Canadians alike, in danger here.

"Look—help me help you guys. You were here trespassing on a Canadian government installation with weapons, and you're carriers. Regulation dictates that we eradicate you." He looked at Dalton and Graham for any sort of reaction and then began bouncing the pencil against the desk again. He dropped the pencil, leaned back, and smoothed his hair back with one hand. He was giving up.

"Fine. Take them back," he commanded the guards. "And you two? Just let the guards know when you're ready to talk."

On the trip back, Graham again tried to map the layout of their surroundings. Once inside, after the guards had left them alone, McCann made eye contact with him and nodded, but said nothing.

"What happened?" Rick whispered.

"They don't know what the hell they're doing," Dalton said. "They're unaware of the terrorists, and from what I can tell they have no communication outside this compound. They've been living in a vacuum all this time."

"Do they know we have a vaccine?" Rick said.

"Clarisse has been interrogated," Dalton smirked, "but I guarantee you Lieutenant Harding is no match for her, and I don't think he got anything from her. From that room we were in, I'm guessing she got more clues about them than we did." He suppressed his laughter.

"What do you think, Graham? Did you find any way out?" Dalton asked.

"No. The place looks industrial. They were walking way too close to us, though—you know? It's like they have no experience with the virus. They must have closed off the town early on and stayed quiet."

"As far as I know, there were no military installations out this way —but then again, I'm not Canadian," Dalton added. If they're going by the rule of law, then yes, we're in violation by their extensive gun laws here, but we were not trespassing. There were no signs of violation. I can't believe we're even debating this considering the circumstances."

"But we didn't exactly show our passports at the border," Reuben said.

"Are they military or militia?" Graham asked.

"That's a good question," Dalton answered.

"Canadians don't have militias. It's against their laws," Sam said.

"Really?" Graham asked.

"Yep," Sam said.

"Hmmm, you get so used to life a certain way that you expect everyone else is playing by the same rules," Graham said.

"What's important is that the rules have changed, and these guys haven't figured that out yet," Sam commented. And that's a real problem."

"Okay. In the meantime, it sounds like the others are fine. I know this is frustrating, but we have to wait them out. If they're still playing by the old rules, it'll take a few days at the most," Dalton advised.

"We'll give it time, then. Stay calm." Graham glanced over at McCann, who hadn't opened his mouth once but spoke volumes now when he managed to roll his blackened, swollen eyes before turning toward the damp wall.

16

Hope

Lieutenant Harding approached his superior's office with a dreadful sense of unease, pausing before reaching for the doorknob. He let out a gale of breath to ready himself and tried to clear his mind. Though they all accredited Captain Gordon with the early action that had saved their lives, the old man was losing his mind. Without question, his policy of absolute quarantine had saved them all, but it came at a significant cost: Gordon had become nothing more than a dictator in the past year, and his ascent to this role was beginning to cause everyone apprehension. Increasingly, any encounter with him brought dread.

Though technically militias were forbidden in Canada, there was an agreement *within* some of the military ranks to act if necessary. This was a militia held secretly by the military but never referred as a militia. It began simply enough, secretly, after 9/11, with meetings held in code and under the cover of night. Plans were hatched to save their families. Each member slowly started relocating to the area or buying summer lots and visited under the pretense of vacationing. Their plans ramped up after the terrorist attack on Parliament Hill in Ottawa, and they added new procedures for every possible scenario.

Once the pandemic broke out they, like most of the prepper survivors, put their plans into place, left their posts, and took over the defensible city of Hope according to their contingency plans for a pandemic. Hope was perfectly isolated, with mountains on one side and lakes on the other. It was a natural castle with a built-in moat.

The citizens of the resort town were at first taken unawares when heavy artillery rolled in and military floatplanes landed. Next they became extremely agitated when the militia put up roadblocks and set up quarantine buildings. Residents were tested and confined to their homes until they were proven disease-free; all those allowed to remain within the town borders were uninfected.

But soon no one was allowed to enter or leave anymore. All communication from the outside world, dying around them, was silenced. They were prepared for a fight from those wanting in, but no one had ever come. Until now.

It worked, but at what cost? We don't even know what's happened to the outside world, Harding thought. He turned the doorknob and entered Gordon's office.

"Hello Henry, what's the report?" Gordon asked without turning to face him. He sat in his squeaky green office chair, staring out the window at the blooming cherry trees lining the lakeshore.

He's in a good mood today.

"Good afternoon, Ed." They called one another by their first names in private only. It was a silent agreement, one that they both appreciated; it kept the hierarchy clear in public but lent a sense of humanity to the private setting.

Harding sat down in the chair across the desk from his senior and waited for the man to break from his zoned vision out the window.

There were days when Harding would wait and acknowledgment never came. He would simply rise from his chair and leave to come back the next day, only to have the same thing happen again. He couldn't blame Ed Gordon. They now lived with a perpetual second-guessing of their past decisions, and at times this put them on a roller coaster of emotions.

But not today. Gordon, nearing seventy, had aged more in the last year than Harding had thought possible. Harding supposed that he himself might have similarly aged, but he hadn't cared to check the mirror lately. Gordon's chair squeaked as he turned to face Harding; it seemed to take a great physical effort. Gordon was like a man climbing reluctantly up a ladder to retrieve his neighbor's wayward Frisbee. Now face to face with Harding across his desk, Gordon's blue eyes were in stark contrast to his aging, pale skin.

"What do they want?" Gordon finally asked, his voice becoming hoarse.

Harding shook his head and let out a small shrug. "That is a good question, Ed. I don't know yet."

"They're in the quarantine housing outside the border, right?"

"Yes, of course. As planned." Harding wasn't certain why his boss would ask that question. It was as if he doubted him.

A thought came to Gordon. "You're sure they're carriers?"

"We're assuming so, of course."

Gordon nodded again. "They have a pregnant one with them, you say?"

"Yes, she looks to be seven to eight months along, though no one has examined her."

"Isn't it odd that we haven't had one birth since this all began? We have three hundred and fifty-two people here. It will be like one of those drought rings in a tree if some archaeologist decides to study us once we're gone."

Harding wasn't sure where Gordon was going with this line of thought when Gordon suddenly pointed a finger at him. "We don't torture them for information. That's against our laws."

"No, of course not. I've questioned one of the women and two of the men. None of them has answered my inquiries. We're still going through their vehicles. They were extremely well prepared. We suspect some of them are prior military. They're in violation of importing firearms into the country and trespassing, but considering the circumstances, I'm not sure we can blame them."

Gordon looked directly at him. "They're deadly to us and the rest of the world. If they have the virus, they must be exterminated. I . . . I hate to do it, but it's a must." He stared back out the window, and Harding knew he'd lost him for now. He began to rise when Gordon surprised him.

"Finish your investigation and get as much information from them as possible, and then euthanize them all as humanely as possible." He gestured with his hand as if to sweep away dust.

Harding stared at the motion, thinking of its callousness. Again he was certain that things were going off track. *What is the point of living this way and taking souls? What gives us the right?* He knew from experience that once Ed shooed you out it was time to leave, so he pulled open the door and exited. There had been a time when he'd argue with Ed Gordon, but the last time that happened Ed had gotten himself into such a state that Henry was afraid the old man might lock him up for treason, or even have him killed.

Now he handled his superior with kid gloves. *Wait until he looks at you. Speak only when spoken to. Don't offend him, and especially don't second-guess his authority or his decisions.* He held great respect for the man, but things were different now. Where Ed Gordon had excelled at saving them before the pandemic took a firm hold on humanity, they now needed someone else to lead them out and into the new world. Only recently had Harding come to the secret conclusion that Gordon would not be that man. They would live and die here, never knowing what happened to the outside world, and to Gordon that conclusion to the story was one of failure. A different day, perhaps, but the same end result: death.

Ed has a point, though, Harding thought as he left the building. *There have been no births since the onset of the pandemic.* Out of the 150 or so women residing in Hope, not one had become pregnant. That meant that no one expected to survive another generation, so why bother? They weren't living, but merely biding their time until death's arrival.

He walked back to his office. The outside air felt cool against his face, and the perfume of spring blossoms floated on a light breeze. He'd planned to let the brunette sit tight for a while, but suddenly he felt an urgent need to get some answers out of her. He didn't want them to die. Not only did they survive but had achieved something his group had not: they were thriving. He needed to find out their story—and quickly, before Gordon called for their demise. He could hold his boss at bay by prolonging the search and questioning period, but for how long could he delay the carrying out of the final order?

17

Frustration

By the second day the dark, damp room was beginning to smell. Though the facilities worked, water leaked from the bathroom tap and drained down along the concrete flooring to the lowest point where it collected it a mildewy pool, so they left the bathroom door open to encourage evaporation.

There were no chairs to sit on, only blankets and pillows that had been brought by the guards and hastily tossed inside right after they arrived. McCann and Sam had been made comfortable on pallets atop the cold concrete flooring; their injuries were not life-threatening, but Graham and the other men needed something to do, and caring for the injured seemed like the task at hand. So far they had not received any rations, and on this second day all woke up hungry, though no one mentioned it.

"Get up, McCann. You need to walk around," Graham said, ignored McCann's protests as he pulled him first into a sitting position and then to a stand.

"I don't care. I don't want to walk around, Graham. I want to get out of here, and—"

"I know. Don't you think I know? Trust me, I'm ready to tear down these walls, but that won't do the girls or us any good."

McCann took in a big breath of stale air and let it out.

"Now get your rear up, McCann. You need to walk around. You might have had internal injuries."

"I don't have internal injuries. They took Macy away unconscious . . . I don't even know if she's alive."

"Hey, look. She's with Clarisse. I'm *sure* she's alive."

"There was a gunshot. I was on the ground. Then *she* was on the ground. Sheriff came out of nowhere. I have no idea what happened to him, either, or Frank and Elsa. Or the horses, for that matter. Most of all, I can't help Macy in here, Graham."

Graham held McCann up and forced him to walk.

"My ears were ringing, and then I passed out. When I came to, Sam was passed out and Macy was gone."

McCann kept to himself most of the time, but now he was worried. Graham could relate: it was killing him not knowing how Tala was faring. She and the kids meant everything to him. If something were to happen to them, this new family he'd grown to love in the past year, he couldn't cope. This time, he'd end it. That level of heartbreak wasn't something someone could go through twice in a lifetime. But he feared that McCann might be contemplating the same; clearly he was in despair.

"McCann, this is a temporary situation. The others are safe. These guys might have escaped the pandemic, but they've done little else to figure out what's happened to the world and how to deal with it. And"—he attempted to make light of their situation—"they're *Canadians*; what harm could come to us?"

"I know you think they're harmless, but I'm pretty sure they've changed a few national policies since the pandemic started," McCann said.

Graham conceded. "You might be right, but still, it doesn't help to worry."

"Look Graham, if they don't bring us rations today, you can bet they don't plan to keep us around. Why waste food on people you intend to kill? If they don't bring us food today, we need to try and escape."

"Let's not jump to conclusions. The day has only just begun," Graham said, but he'd already had thoughts along the same lines. If no food came by the end of the day, the Canadians would find out who they were dealing with.

"He's right," Sam said from his spot on the ground.

"Quiet!" Dalton yelled. He was on watch through the cracks in the door and was trying in vain to hear beyond the conversations in the room.

McCann and Graham walked forward and tried to look as well. Graham spotted one of their own supply trucks parked at a little brick building across the street. There were voices coming from the other side of the truck. As Graham focused on them suddenly, two yellow-clad guards came striding from the left with Clarisse handcuffed between them.

"Hey! There's Clarisse!" Dalton said, his voice rising in excitement.

"So it's a good guess they're being kept somewhere in that direction," McCann concluded.

"Yep. And she seems fine. She wouldn't walk so well, and so willingly, otherwise. She's taking long strides, she's relaxed. She looks in control. They're probably bringing her in for more questioning," Dalton said. They watched as she disappeared around another building with her escorts.

"Damn," Dalton said, but nothing more.

18

Barter

Clarisse sat in the steel chair as she had the day before. Harding was waiting behind the glass partition, but didn't look up when she entered the room. She didn't expect to be back here so soon, thinking they were in for a few days of isolation.

The most pressing issue was food for Tala and the children. They had access to water, but food was a pressing matter, and she worried about Tala's blood sugar levels. Harding's games needed to end, or the lack of food intake could have permanent consequences on an unborn child.

And Olivia had nothing to do other than to comfort the children. She was beginning to go a little crazy. Watching hungry children in pain isn't something a mother handles well, and Clarisse wasn't sure how much longer Olivia could keep it together.

Finally, Harding looked up at her. *Let the games begin.*

"Hello, Ms. . . . ?"

She smiled.

"Oh, that's right. You're not talking." He smiled a little too smugly, which made her think he might know something she didn't. "That's all right. I already know your name. You're Dr. Clarisse Smarting." He then dangled her military ID from its lanyard.

Dammit. It must have fallen off during the scuffle.

"It says here you're a virologist. I still have many unanswered questions, however. Like, what are *these*?" He held up several USB sticks containing her vaccination formula. "We took a look at the files inside and the information appears to be some kind of recipe. Are those vaccine vials in the refrigerated case?"

She wished she could consult with Dalton. Harding might push her into divulging something or making a decision that would affect the whole group. She stared past his head through the glass at the laboratory behind him.

Her voice came through, though not as loud as she'd have liked it to, not as commanding. "Like I said yesterday, I have something you want."

"Are you saying you have a cure for the China Flu?" There was a difference now in Harding's tone. She'd expected him to be condescending—triumphant, even—but he wasn't. Instead, he spoke with what sounded like compassion.

"No. I'm saying I have a *vaccine* for the China Flu."

He looked confused. "Your people aren't carriers?"

"Some are."

Harding dropped his pencil on the table, "Which ones?"

She shook her head. "I won't tell you; I won't let you use them as pawns. Some of them are carriers of the virus, and some have been inoculated against it. They may or may not be virulent, but that no longer matters to the rest of us."

Harding leaned back in his chair, then sat up again. "You're telling me you developed a vaccine for this virus?"

Clarisse nodded.

"It's efficient, it produces antibodies?"

She nodded again.

Harding digested this new information. He couldn't believe their luck. He ran a hand through his hair and then frowned suddenly. "Wait— that does us no good. You only have around twenty vials of the vaccine, and we have over three hundred and fifty people here." He sat back, looking devastated; he'd been too quick to dream of a resolution and was now visibly drained.

Clarisse was about to broaden his horizons. "That's not a problem. I can make more."

He looked at her skeptically. "How do I know that what you say is the truth?"

She couldn't think of a thing to convince him. "You don't. You might just have to *trust* me on this."

"Have you used the vaccine on your people?"

"Yes."

"Did any of them die as a result?"

"No."

Harding paused a moment to think.

"Have you ever knowingly infected anyone?"

"You're reaching now. If you let us go, I'll create enough vaccine for your people."

"Answer the question."

"Of course not. I'm a doctor. I took an oath. We're not evil, but you're putting yourself—and us—in danger by keeping us locked up like this. There are things going on out there that you don't know about."

"Tell me."

"No. Let my people go, and then we'll talk. Keep us prisoner and someone else could expose you. Or worse, someone may come and overrun this place."

Tap, tap, tap . . .

"I don't have the final say," Harding finally answered. "I'll talk to my boss."

Clarisse began to rise from the chair. "Keep those refrigerated if you want any hope at all. This meeting is over." She walked to the door again and patiently waited for the guard to open it.

19

Not Hopeful

"I'm telling you, Ed. She can do it," Harding said.

Ed Gordon had turned away to face the window a few minutes ago when he knew the argument was failing. In the process, he'd blocked Harding out.

"This isn't living, Ed. These people of ours, they are as much prisoners as the folks we have locked up out there. As you yourself have pointed out, the birthrate is at zero. There are no marriages. The last three deaths we've had have all been suicides, and they were all just this month; they're killing themselves rather than live through this. Next winter more and more will die. We're living like zombies, Ed. If, we can become vaccinated, we can at least become immune to the virus. We need to give our people hope and then get out there and see what's happening to our world, try to start over again. And the same for these people we have in lockup."

Convincing Ed was no use; he'd shut down, wouldn't respond.

The man was sick, and it was about time he recognized that about himself. Ed would rather keep these people locked up, to die slowly, than to heal them.

With boiling rage, Harding brushed his hair back into place, picked up his papers, and tried to lower his tone to one of civility. "You're incompetent, Ed. This"—he gestured around the room—"this is some sort of sick denial. We have a chance to beat this thing, and I can't let you euthanize these people because you're uncomfortable with the outside world. I'm letting them go. I'm going to let Dr. Smarting create the vaccine for us—even help her if I can. And after that, I'm letting them go on their way. You can stay here if you'd like, stay in this room, alone, for all I care. But the rest of us need space, maybe freedom if it's out there." He left Gordon's office, and for the first time, he didn't close the door behind him as he'd been trained to do.

AN HOUR LATER, Harding had closed up his office for the night and just stepped outside the building when he heard a gunshot. He dived to the road, landing hard, and the gravel tore at his flesh. His papers flew into the air around him, then drifted like graceful birds to the ground. Guards were running everywhere. *Have the prisoners escaped?*

"Sir!"

Harding pushed himself to his knees. "What? What happened?"

"The major, sir. Self-inflicted," the guards said.

A wave of nausea hit him. "Ed's dead?"

"Yes, sir," the guard said. "Completely."

"You're in charge now, sir. What should we do?"

He gathered his papers, attempting to tap them into a neat pile on the gravel road. "Was there a note? I just left him a little while ago."

"No, sir. No note."

The guard's radio broke the silence. "Orders? Over."

"Um . . . get him cleaned up," Harding commanded. "Have a grave dug. I'll make an announcement soon." He avoided eye contact with the guard. *I did this. I pushed Ed too far.*

Harding walked back to his office. Several other guards rushed past him, gravel crunching under their boots as they ran and the spent petals of tree blossoms drifted toward the ground. Part of him felt released; the other part felt responsible.

20

A Solution

"Look, it's been two days since we heard the shot. We don't know what the hell is going on," McCann complained.

"They brought us food, at least," Graham said.

"But they won't answer our questions. They won't even tell us if the girls are okay." McCann paced the floor for what seemed like the millionth time, and Graham was having an increasingly difficult time getting him to remain calm. He was scared too—hell, they all were. But there was nothing to gain by causing problems.

"We watched Clarisse return. She was fine. She wasn't upset. Then we heard a single shot later that afternoon," Graham said. "That doesn't mean anything bad. It could have been a deer, for all we know."

"Then we saw a lot of running. That was a lot of excitement for a deer. Or they could have put one of the dogs down," McCann said, stopping in his tracks.

"Still, there's nothing we can do about it right now." Graham reasoned.

They were so focused on their argument that they barely heard the lock trip and the door open.

"Hello, gentlemen. We would like you two to come with us. The lieutenant would like to speak with you."

"Let us go!" McCann yelled, and Sam jumped up and pushed McCann backward to keep him from charging the guards.

"McCann, stop!" Graham said. "You're not helping!"

"They can't just keep us here!" McCann yelled.

Surprisingly, one of the guards held up one of his hands and said, "It won't be for much longer."

"What is that supposed to mean?" McCann said.

The other guard looked at his comrade and shook his head without saying anything more. "Look, I've said too much. Please come with us."

Graham was up, and as Dalton stood slowly, he brushed his hands on the back of his pants to wipe off the damp gravel. Coughing as if to emphasize his point, he said, "We're all getting sick in this damp cell you've got us in."

Neither guard commented as they were led out. The bright afternoon sun burned their eyes. Graham had started to notice that Dalton appeared to be declining; he wasn't yet healed from the bear attack or their scrap with the invaders. The cold damp room they were kept in caused them all to shiver at night and even huddling together didn't keep their hands and feet from going almost numb with cold.

Something has to happen—today, Graham thought.

When they entered the room, the one thing they hadn't thought to expect was Clarisse standing there. And she looked as shocked as they did.

Clarisse started toward Dalton, but he shook his head subtly. It wasn't a good idea to show them who your loved ones were; information like that could be used against you.

"Didn't expect to see you here, Dr. Smarting," Dalton said, trying to sound formal, and Graham looked around to see who he was addressing before it came to him that it was Clarisse. He didn't recall having ever heard her last name before now. Graham caught on that they were probably being watched, and soon the door opened on the other side of the glass window and Lieutenant Harding entered.

"Hello, folks. Sorry I'm late. I thought we could talk a little about our situation here. Please have a seat." He gestured toward three chairs on their side of the glass, and the three sat.

Harding cleared his throat. "Our situation has changed here. I needn't go into the details, but we're willing to let you go—*if* Dr. Smarting can develop enough vaccine for the people of Hope."

"You'll release us while she's developing the vaccine?" Dalton asked.

"No. That's too dangerous. I'll release the women and children while she's developing the vaccine. I'll hold the rest of you until she's completed her work and then you'll be set free. Deal?"

"You bastard! No deal," Clarisse said. "You'll release *all* of us. We can't trust you. You've imprisoned us against our will, and we have not committed any crime against you." Graham had never seen Clarisse this pissed off, but she had a good point.

"Wait," Dalton called out for calm. "You want the vaccine, but you want to hold onto something to ensure that Clar . . . Dr. Smarting completes her end of the bargain?"

"That's about right, yeah," Harding answered.

Dalton leaned forward and pointed at the glass. "That's pretty evil of you guys. We'd be willing to share the vaccine with you, but this kind of treatment tells us quite a bit about your nature. There's a lot you don't know about what's going on out in the real world, and you need to get a grip. You're not safe here in your little hidey-hole. Not for long, anyway. We came here to get away from danger, and once we figure out how to fight it, we're going back. This is just temporary. Now, you can treat us like prisoners, but let me tell you something: you *need* us. We should be allies, not enemies."

Harding ignored Dalton's warning. "We've set up housing right outside of town for you. The women and children will be set free.

The men can move into what is presently the women's prison; it has heating, and you'll find the accommodations are far better than in your current setup. As for this danger you keep alluding to, you need to get to the point. We are not defenseless here, sir, and I don't know what gave you that impression. Despite your ammunition and expertise, we took you down quite easily, did we not?"

"You took a tired group by surprise. Congratulations." Dalton conceded.

"What about Mark and McCann?" Graham asked. He hadn't spoken yet, but wanted to find out who Harding considered children, and whether he could get the two young men free.

"The women will need hunters to bring in food," said Graham. "I have two boys in the men's prison that should go with them." He was lying in hopes that Harding would believe McCann was eighteen.

"How old are they?"

"One is seventeen; the other is eighteen."

He wrote something down on a piece of paper. "Anyone under the age of eighteen can go—but not that young man who gave my guards hell, regardless of his age. He stays with you, and the doctor here stays with us."

"No, that's not possible," protested Clarisse. "We have a pregnant woman with us, and I need to monitor her. I'll reside with the women and children and come to the lab every day on my own. I won't try to escape—you have my word. I wouldn't leave without the rest of the group anyway."

Harding stopped writing and looked up at her. "You won't try to escape?" he asked.

Clarisse shook her head. "As long as the prisoners are treated fairly. They need food and water, and they need humane treatment. I also want the right to visit with them once a day." She was pushing it —asking for more than she guessed Harding would allow.

"No. You can see them once a week to monitor their condition and give them updates on your progress. No more than that. Are we clear?"

"Can you and I discuss this in private?"

"Look, you're getting to set half your party free in exchange for the development of the vaccine. When the vaccine is viable, the rest of you may go."

"You're still ignoring the greater threat here," Graham said.

"Sir, at the moment I have individuals in my midst who could bring death to my door. At the same time, they have the power to save every citizen here. I'm bargaining with them, I'm feeding them, and I think that's pretty reasonable. At the moment you are both my biggest threat and my greatest hope.

"I suspect the problem you are alluding to is political in nature. Your country has finally taken advantage of a good tragedy. *Never let a good tragedy go to waste?* Who was it that said that? The conservative against the liberal factions, and they are both fighting over what's left of your country. A civil war? We've heard about the same dilemma in our own. That's why we shut off all communications from the outside, because in the end it doesn't matter. It astounds me how politics is the ruination of mankind."

"That's not it. You're wrong," Dalton said.

"It's actually much worse," Graham added.

"If it is, then stop playing games and tell me what it is. What do I have to be so worried about now that most of humanity is dead? What more could happen?"

"The virus . . . wasn't caused by the Chinese. It only began there," Clarisse interjected.

"*What?*"

"It was Islamic terrorists. Jihadists," Dalton answered. "They caused this and they're here now; on this continent. Only a few hours away, in fact."

All color drained from Harding's face, and he took up his pencil again.

Tap, tap, tap . . .

21

A Visit

"How are the boys?" Dalton asked. This was the longest he'd gone without seeing them since being deployed many years ago in that giant sandbox built called the Middle East.

"They're fine. They miss you, but I keep reassuring them that we'll all be together soon. Kade's threatening to break you out of prison," she said with a smile.

He loved that smile. He didn't like the dark circles under her eyes —she'd been working too many hours, night and day—but the smile was good. Dalton pictured little Kade springing them from jail and thought about how much he missed his sons. "How much longer do you think until you have enough of the vaccine developed?"

Clarisse looked behind her at the guard. "Could you give us some privacy?"

"Sorry, ma'am. My orders are to witness all communications between you and the prisoners."

She shook her head. "I had a feeling you were going to say that. The vaccine development is coming along fine. Luckily, they kept all of my equipment intact. Their lab isn't as good as mine was, but I'm managing." She brightened at imparting the next bit of information. "And they kept the horses and chickens; we have them now, and they're doing fine. Macy insisted on taking over the horses. Unfortunately, the dogs ran off during the big kerfuffle, and no one has seen them since."

"So we don't know if Sheriff was shot?" Graham asked.

"I've asked about that. The guard who fired said he didn't know. He couldn't guess if Sheriff caught the shot or not, only that he ran off into the woods."

"And how's Tala?" Graham asked.

"She's great. She"—Clarisse whispered so that the guard couldn't hear her words—"she sends her love."

Graham nodded. "It's been two weeks. I'm afraid she's going to have the baby without me there."

"She's got another three weeks or so to go, I think. I'll be done before then, and you'll be there."

"Time's up!" the guard announced.

Dalton knew it wasn't wise, but he couldn't help himself—he reached for Clarisse's hand and held her. "Please hurry, if you can."

"I'm trying. We're almost there, and . . . I have the beginning of an idea." She looked him in the eye and became very serious. "It's a dreadful solution, but it *is* a solution," Clarisse said quietly.

The guard walked her way and reached for her arm.

"Sorry. Time to go, eh?" the guard said.

"Tell me about it the next time you visit," Dalton said and pressed a kiss into the back of her hand before the guard took her away.

"WHAT WAS SHE TALKING ABOUT?" Graham asked Dalton after Clarisse and the guard had left.

"I think she mean's she's figured out how to defeat the terrorists.

That means either she's found equipment here that we might be able to fight with, or . . . she said *dreadful*. It means she has a way to exterminate them. Your guess is as good as mine, but if she said it, it's for real."

Just then Rick strolled out of the steamy bathroom. "Man, it's nice to have a hot shower. Did Clarisse leave? What'd I miss?"

Neither Dalton nor Graham answered, so McCann chimed in. "We're getting out of here in another two weeks, and Clarisse has a plan to kill the terrorists. Oh, and Macy is fine. She's taking care of the horses and chickens."

"Said the King of Summary," Graham added.

"Seriously? That's good news!" said Rick.

"Looks that way," Dalton added, "but we have no idea what she has in mind yet, so don't get your hopes up. Clarisse only said she has the *beginning* of an idea,"

"Are we expecting a visit from the lieutenant today?" Rick asked.

"I don't know, Rick. I haven't checked our busy agenda for the day."

"Aw, don't get all pissy on me, Dalton," Rick said and pointed at him while explaining to Graham, "he doesn't do captivity very well."

Dalton tried to hide his grin.

"He tends to get claustrophobic. Somewhat like our young friend here." Rick went to ruffle McCann's hair, but the murderous look the young man gave him stopped him in his tracks. "No?"

Dalton and Graham both laughed and then Dalton mused, "What the hell—did anyone see this coming? We're being held hostage until our brilliant scientist Clarisse can create enough vaccine for our jailers. In the meantime, our true enemy is inching its way farther across the United States with the idea of taking over the world. I don't know about you guys, but I never saw *that* coming."

"I'm rather enjoying the captivity myself," Rick said. "We get to sleep all day in dry beds, and they deliver food to us. Welcome to the Postapocalypse Hotel."

Graham couldn't help but be amused, and with Rick's latest comment even McCann was smiling. They needed this. Maybe it was a sign of insanity, but Graham knew their long-term survival depended on some level of humor from time to time.

"We could escape," McCann said quietly.

"Dalton stopped laughing and turned his eyes to McCann. "Son, I've been watching everything as much as you have. Yes, the guards are sloppier each day than they were the day before. We could easily overpower them. Only one guard comes in now, and he's loaded down with food trays, his gun slung over his back. Yes, we could escape. But as much as we want to be with the ones we love, escaping would put them in danger.

"I don't think it would take much for one of these guys to pull the trigger, do you? They're scared of us. Are you willing to risk one of our few loved ones because you're tired of being locked up? Huh? How about Bethany, or Lucy. Or maybe Mark, or even Macy. You willing to take that chance?"

McCann cleared his throat and leaned against the cold cinderblock wall, pressing his skin against the coldness—anything to feel something instead of numb. He didn't want them to, but Dalton's words made sense to him.

"Answer me, McCann! Because if you're willing to put *any* of them in danger, I need to know!" Dalton shook with anger now.

McCann's eyes widened. He'd never seen Dalton this angry, and he knew he'd gone too far. "No. It's an option, that's all," he said.

"No. It's *not* an option until I say so," Dalton shot back.

Sam tried to lighten the ensuing painful quiet, "McCann, we've all thought it. We have a plan right now where no one gets killed. Let's stick with this strategy unless something changes."

Dalton softened his tone to one that bordered on apology. "McCann, you have to understand that we can't afford to lose anyone. Not *one*. Do you get that?"

"Yeah, I get it. I just don't think they're going to keep their end of the bargain, that's all. We don't negotiate with terrorists, right? What about hostage takers? That's what they are. We've done nothing wrong. They took us prisoner, and now we're negotiating with them. Doesn't that seem screwed up to you?"

To ease the tension, Graham spoke before Dalton had another chance. "McCann, yes, this is a screwed-up situation. No, they were not right to take us hostage, but they have their reasons. We're going to vaccinate them against the flu. That's a good thing; it will save their lives. They're human beings trying to survive, just like us, and despite their lousy way of showing humanity, we're doing the right thing. We need as many people on our side as we can get right now. Don't you agree?"

McCann nodded.

"In the meantime, we are all on forced rest for the next two weeks. Let's take advantage of it. We're all healing from different injuries. At least the rest of our group are living in real housing and doing well. Mark is with them; Macy is taking care of the horses. Everything is going to work out, McCann. Just hang in there."

McCann nodded again. As each man settled quietly into his own world, Graham watched as McCann lay down again and rolled over to face the wall. It was only a matter of time before the young man would do something to endanger them all. He needed to get him outside. Perhaps he'd talk to the lieutenant before it was too late.

22

An Escort

Clarisse was startled by a knock on the lab door. "Yes, come in," she said.

Lieutenant Harding walked through the entrance, his dark hair combed perfectly. "Hello, Clarisse. I see you're working overtime. Come, I'll walk you back to housing."

She continued to stare through her microscope. He'd been getting a little too comfortable with her lately. He would occasionally touch the small of her back or grab her elbow to lead her in some direction. Even though these were only small gestures, the physical contact bothered her. She suspected he was a lonely man, even as handsome as he was. Inasmuch as she realized she could use this to her advantage, she tried not to show her distaste for Harding.

Not that he was bad looking; he just wasn't Dalton. No one but Dalton could ever make her feel anything with a touch. The problem was, this was an advantage, and she needed to use it no matter how much it made her want to gag.

She pasted a smile on her face and turned to him. "Hello, Lieutenant."

"Please, we talked about this. Call me Henry," he said with a charming smile.

"Yes, of course—Henry. I'm nearly done. Just let me clean up." Clarisse slipped a USB stick into her lab coat pocket while broadening her smile in hopes it would distract him.

After collecting her things, she exited the building with him close by. "It's nearly dark already. I had no idea it was this late," she said.

"Yes, you'd work around the clock if someone didn't keep track of you."

Oh, please, gag me now.

"It's nothing new. I often keep long hours."

"So, you're nearly done, then?" Harding asked with what almost sounded like disappointment.

"Yes, I've checked and rechecked the vaccine for the same strong antibodies. It works. I'm just sorry I hadn't found it sooner. So many lives have been lost."

The cool evening breeze made her shiver. He wrapped his arm around her and pulled her toward him while brushing her arms back and forth to warm her. He was a sweet man, but she was beginning to feel a bit nauseated.

"You're amazing, Clarisse," he whispered looking down at her.

Horror struck as she thought he might take the initiative and attempt to kiss her. She took a step forward out of his embrace and quickly said, "No. I'm just a little cold. I can make it the rest of the way. Thank you, Henry."

He let her go. "Good night, Clarisse. See you tomorrow."

She quickly made her way to the guard standing by the fenced enclosure where three small houses stood. Macy stood with one of the horses, brushing her mane as Clarisse approached.

"I saw that. Was he touching you? Are you okay?" Macy asked, eyes wide.

"Yes. Gather everyone and come inside. I have something to say."

CLARISSE CLEARED the kitchen table of the final scraps left over from their evening meal. Everyone gathered in the dining room while Mark watched the front door, and Bang and Hunter guarded the back door.

"Did you get the computer?" Clarisse asked Olivia.

"Yes, we snuck into the truck and pulled it out after promising the guards cookies. It's amazing what these guys will do for a little real food and a few fresh eggs."

"Yeah, well"—Clarisse pulled out the USB stick—"I've got something to confess." She looked around the room as if to check for someone listening. "I finished the vaccine a week ago."

"What? Why would you keep something like that a secret?" asked Macy.

"Shhh," Mark admonished. "I'm sure she has her reasons. Let her explain."

They all stared at her.

"Yes," Clarisse nodded, "I do have a reason. I wasn't certain at first, but now I am. I was in the lab and thinking about how we might stop the jihadists. I've had an idea, and I needed the lab to research the possibilities." She held up the USB stick.

"You know how I developed the vaccine for the China virus? Well, my vaccine has specific markers. Mostly in the adjuvant I used to stabilize it. It's different from any other vaccine ever developed. If you were to look at the antibodies under a microscope, you'd see it has its own thumbprint. You could identify it from its components and tell it apart from any other.

"The terrorists have a vaccine too, one they made and delivered only to those they chose—only their terrorist allies. It's also unique, with markers different from the one I developed. Follow me?"

Clarisse looked around. She could tell Macy had already leaped to the next stage but was biding her time until everyone else clued up. *Good girl.*

"My theory was, if I could make"—Clarisse's voice lowered to an even quieter tone—"a highly virulent, mutated virus that targeted a specific blueprint in those that received their vaccine, we could infect only them."

Silence filled the room.

"That would be genocide." Lucy's voice quavered. "I . . . I . . . I'm not saying I'm against it. After all, that's what they're trying to do to us. I'm just calling it what it is, that's all."

Clarisse nodded. "That's exactly what I'm saying, Lucy. That's why I'm talking to you all. I've figured out how to do it, though I need test subjects. I wasn't completely sure if it was even a viable solution, but it is. Science is dangerous in the wrong hands, we've found that out the hard way. This . . . is a way to change what they set into motion.

"Yes, it's genocide, but what choice do we have? The jihadists have taken all choice from us. At this point it's survival of the fittest—those with the knowledge to make the biggest bomb or the most heinous piece of science—like this, like a virus that will kill based on certain markers. I'm asking you to let me continue my research for another week under the guise of completing the vaccines for our captors. I'll accept the responsibility for genocide if it works."

"You don't have to do that, Clarisse. We're in this together," Macy said. Murmurs all around agreed. "So the men will have to stay captive for another week. Then what?"

Clarisse swallowed hard. She knew what this meant. She wasn't sure if she could live with herself afterward, but she could until the time came.

"I tell Dalton. We try to get these guys to help us. We need to capture a few terrorists for test subjects. I'll extract the antibodies from them, locate the markers, and then develop the virus. It's much more complicated than I can share accurately. We'll then inject them with it, send them back out into the wild, and let the virus take hold."

Mark left the doorway and walked over to the group. "How long do you think it will take to spread?"

"I don't know for sure. Not long, I would imagine."

"Can we get a message to the guys to let them know what we're planning? I know they must be going crazy in there," Macy said.

"We can't take any chances," Tala said. She turned to Clarisse. "Are you sure this virus would only affect those with the specific markers they've used?"

Clarisse watched as Tala moved her hand over the child within her swollen belly. *My God, what am I doing?* She shook her head. "I can't be one hundred percent sure until I have test subjects to work with. For example, I can't guarantee the virus I make won't mutate into something else in time. It's a risk we take. It's the same for them; they created this virus, and it may mutate into something else entirely in years to come, or it may disappear. Once it's released, it's up to the whims of nature. We have no control after that. We can only try to come up with another vaccine to counter that one specific virus. Does everyone understand why this is taking so long? That's why I need another week to work out how I might come up with this virus. It's like the reverse of the process I created for the vaccine."

"Yes," Tala said, "and I understand what a massive amount of pressure you're under. I take it the guys don't know about this at all?"

"No. The guard is always present when I'm visiting them. I've tried to drops hints to Dalton, but we're observed very closely. The men don't know what's going on, and we need to keep it that way for now. In another week, I'll have a more specific plan worked out. We don't know if Harding and his people will let us use their lab after they have their vaccine. That's why we need to pull this little ruse for one more week, and that's why I needed this computer. I can work here in the evening."

Tala could see the stress was wearing on Clarisse. She agreed this was the best plan they had so far. "We can handle it, right guys? One more week. Stay patient. Keep your heads, and no heroic moves." She aimed her eyes at Mark and the twins, who were always scheming when the adults weren't looking.

Everyone began to disperse when Clarisse thought of one more thing. "Hey Macy, still no sign of Sheriff or the other dogs?"

Macy's hopeful face turned to one of sorrow in an instant. "No. One of the guards even let me go back to the road. There was some blood—not a lot. I'm not sure if it was McCann's, mine, or Sheriff's.

Lucy and I've walked through the woods calling for all three of them. Nothing. It's like they vanished."

"I'm sure he'll turn up. Let's not give up hope," Clarisse said. She chastised herself for bringing it up. *The poor girl had managed to put her sorrow aside for a moment, and I had to remind her of it again.*

AFTER EVERYONE HAD GONE to bed, Clarisse stayed up at the kitchen table going through her data. *Can you really do this? Commit murder on a massive scale?* The thought nagged at her no matter how she tried to push it from her mind. But then she flashed on the image of Dutch fighting in the last moments of is life as the terrorists chanted and danced around him. And how the families of those in quarantine died before her eyes with nothing she could do to save them. It had to stop. *It's their extinction or ours.* She had a way to stop them; she just needed a little time to figure out the specifics—and patience to deal with Harding and his misguided affections.

23

Still Missing

"Don't go alone," Tala said.

Macy had thought she could sneak past Tala at dawn. "But I *like* going alone. I've got to find Sheriff and the other dogs. And why are you up so early?"

Tala smiled at her. Macy was a master of deflection. "The baby keeps me up. And don't try to change the subject, Macy. It's for your safety, you know. You must have someone with you when you're out there. What if one of the guards thinks you're a target?" Tala attempted to get up off the couch, but in her very pregnant state it was quite a task, and all she could manage was to sit up.

Macy came to help her after noticing her struggle and laughed.

"Don't laugh. This will be you some day," Tala warned.

"Oh, no . . . not me. I'm not doing *that*," Macy said.

"Okay." Tala chuckled. She knew all too well that Macy would change her mind someday. Holding onto the girl's arm, she made it to a standing position. "Seriously, Macy, we can't afford any accidents. Please go get Marcy, or Lucy, or even Bang, and *then* go. Okay?"

Reluctantly Macy wandered off toward the bedrooms. Tala assumed she'd go for Bang first since he was usually up the earliest and because the boy was very much like Macy; they were quiet and comfortable in each other's company. But Macy emerged a few moments later with Lucy in tow; bleary-eyed, but dressed and ready to go. "Good morning, Lucy."

"Good morning, Tala."

"You're up early."

"Yeah. I didn't sleep much last night. I dreamed we were running. Something chased us."

"Well, I can understand that," Macy said. "You ready?"

"Yes."

"Don't stay out too long. I'll worry," Tala said.

After they had gone out into the cool morning air, Tala wondered, *Why Lucy?* Not that the girls didn't get along—they were polite enough to one another—but Macy had at first avoided her. It had seemed at the time that Macy was watching Lucy and deciding whether or not to befriend her. What was this way of life doing to them all? But it couldn't be helped. Out of necessity these children would grow up with a completely different skill set from that of the previous generation. Tala wondered again how her unborn child would grow up in this new and completely different world, one much less populated and much more dangerous.

She yawned and decided she might get another hour of sleep before the day officially started. She'd been up since four, when Clarisse had left for the lab. They'd talked briefly then about having the men home this time tomorrow. The option of genocide weighed heavily on Clarisse. They were nearing the end of the weeks' time limit, and she was going to finish cleaning up her research so that she could let Lieutenant Harding know that the vaccines were finished. They'd agreed that they would all remain in the housing outside of town after the men were released until Clarisse could verify the strong antibodies in all of the citizens of the town of Hope. No plans had been made beyond that; they'd decided to leave their options open.

Tala went to her room and lowered herself onto the bed. Here, in Hope, was the first time she'd slept in a room alone in a very long time. At first she couldn't sleep at all and got up several times to check on Bang, who shared a room with Dalton's boys; Addy slept with Clarisse for the time being.

Tala rolled to her side and ran her hand along the space in the bed that Graham would fill soon. She missed him. Even now, weeks later, she barely slept without him at her side. She didn't feel safe.

She'd felt a few squeezing pains in her belly the last few days. However, Clarisse had dark circles under her eyes and only slept three or four hours a night, and she didn't want to alarm her friend with minor aches and pains.

24

Sprung

There was a light spring hailstorm as Clarisse walked the winding concrete path to Harding's office. Small ice pellets pelted her in the head, remaining in her hair when she entered the lieutenant's building.

She stood before his desk wiping her eyeglasses when she announced, "It's all complete. I have four hundred vials, enough to include anyone else who wanders into camp. I advise you to keep those inoculated quarantined for two weeks until the antibodies take hold. I'll randomly test a group before leaving, but we had no issues with immunity the last time. I don't anticipate any problems." She remembered to smile as she put her glasses back on.

Harding watched her every move with a look of admiration and desire.

Clarisse cleared her throat. "When might we release the men?"

He stood up and smiled broadly. "I cannot tell you how thankful I am," he said, shaking her hand. "I never thought it would be possible to find a cure. We were all so desperate, and then people just started dying off. We escaped and closed down our borders just in time."

He hadn't answered her question. She was beginning to get angry. "The men, Henry. When will they be released?"

"Oh, I already gave the order for their release this afternoon," he checked his watch. "They should be back at your quarters by the time you get back." He smiled, knowing he'd surprised her. "Clarisse, I always keep my promises and I'm sorry we took you prisoner," he said solemnly as he walked around to sit on the front edge of his desk to be nearer to her.

Dalton's home? It was the only thing she could think of.

Harding clasped her hand and ran his thumb over her soft skin, peering into her eyes.

"You've worked around the clock for them. I know they mean a great deal to you. You can rest now, Clarisse. You can stay here, in Hope. In two weeks, your people can join ours, here, with us. We lost our doctor; you can replace him, you're far more qualified . . ." His voice trailed off. She wasn't even looking at him.

He stopped his caress, turning the gesture into a handshake, and smiled broadly to mask his feelings. Perhaps he could tell she wasn't interested. "It's an offer. I hope you'll consider it even if your people decide to leave. *You* can always stay here in Hope—with us."

Clarisse pulled her hand away and finally looked at him. "That's very kind of you, Henry. I'll talk to the others and see what they want to do. We'll begin inoculating everyone tomorrow. I didn't sleep much last night. Would you mind?"

He stood up from the desk and opened the door for her. "Of course not, Clarisse. Rest as long as you want. We'll see each other tomorrow."

Once outside Harding's office, Clarisse realized she'd been holding her breath a good part of the time. Henry was a sweet man, but his charm was misplaced. As she took in a deep breath, her walk turned into a run even though her exhaustion made her unsteady. She slid a few times on the road, now wet from the melted hail. An imaginary cord pulled her to Dalton; she couldn't close the distance fast enough.

DALTON WAITED, pacing restlessly. "Should I go find her?" he asked Graham.

"No, that might cause problems. Be patient. She'll be here soon."

Dalton nodded and swung Kade high up into the beautiful spring air and then pulled him in and hugged him tightly. Hunter wasn't as comfortable as he used to be with his dad loving on him, especially in front of others. Dalton hugged him anyway, but let him loose as soon as he resisted. "You and I need to spend some time together, buddy," he said. Hunter had his mother's eyes, and they pierced Dalton as the boy asked, "What did you do to be put in prison, Dad?"

Dalton held Hunter's small hand and looked to Tala for answers, but she only smiled sympathetically.

"Son, I did nothing wrong. These people, they wanted the vaccine Clarisse could make to keep them from getting sick. So they decided the best way to have her do that, was to keep the other men and me, in holding until she finished making it. I did nothing wrong. I broke no laws."

The boy still looked at him as if trying to decide whether or not to believe him. It was unnerving for Dalton to have his six-year-old son question his honor. Though he knew in this life he'd done some bad things, he'd had to, to keep them going. Would his son judge him harshly for those actions of love and survival? Only time would tell.

As Hunter ran off, Dalton worried that the boy might be fighting internal battles, ones he may have caused. He vowed to spend more time with his son at the first opportunity.

In the meantime, he took advantage of Kade's willingness to let him hold him. Kade was four years old and had yet to outgrow affection from his father. He had especially craved it after his mother's death, and Dalton never denied the boy's cuddles, knowing full well that they were fleeting and would give way to other things little boys grew into. Soon Kade was limp in his arms, and he held the sleeping boy's back against him as he stood outside in the sunshine waiting for a glimpse of Clarisse. "What if they took her into custody in exchange?" he whispered to Graham and Tala. Bang held Graham tightly, as if he'd never let him go again.

Tala smiled at Dalton. "It's too soon to speculate. Clarisse is usually not back until much later—after dark, even—but I expect that once she hears you guys were released she'll come running home."

"*Home?*" Dalton said. He wasn't sure he liked the sound of that. They weren't staying here for very long. "Home is back in Cascade, as far as I'm concerned. This is just temporary."

"Yes, of course. But we women and children have come to consider Hope to be home lately—at least for the time being. Of course, you who were imprisoned probably feel otherwise."

"I know Clarisse has been working on something, but we never got the chance to discuss it. Any idea?" Dalton said.

Tala looked stunned. "You mean, you don't know?"

Both Graham and Dalton looked at her. "Know what? What is she doing? Tell me!" Dalton said.

"I—I shouldn't. It's hers to tell. She'll be here soon, I'm sure." Tala began to walk away, but Graham pulled her back. "We can wait," he said.

At that moment Bang looked up at Graham and blurted out, "Clarisse is going to kill the terrorists with a shot."

"*What?*" Graham asked.

Bang's answer wasn't too far off, but the guys needed clarification, so Tala filled them in. "She's developed a virus that will spread to only those that have the markers of the vaccine they received for the China Flu."

"Are you *serious*?" Graham asked.

Tala nodded.

Dalton said nothing. *A brilliant, deadly idea*, he thought, *but at what cost to Clarisse?*

"I wonder how we're going to pull that off," Graham said. Hail began to fall again, and Graham pulled Tala and Bang inside the house. When he looked back, Dalton stood there, still holding a sleeping Kade against his chest. Graham went back outside and, without a word, took the sleeping child and brought him inside.

Dalton stood there under the hail, waiting for Clarisse and knowing she had to be tormented by what she planned to do, what they'd all have to do, to save themselves and the other survivors. It meant becoming a ruthless beast, just like the jihadists, and Dalton hated the thought of it. But he hated more the idea that Clarisse would condemn herself for finding their salvation.

Soon, he saw her, running toward him through the blizzard of hail. He ran to her too, catching in her shivering form in an embrace. So much to say, and yet nothing needed saying right now.

"God, I've missed you," he finally said into her damp hair. He held her tight to try and give her some of his warmth.

She squeezed him. "Dalton, I . . ." she faltered, crying into his chest.

"I know," he whispered with a wretched pain in his voice.

She convulsed in his arms as the hail came down harder, the little white balls of ice embedding themselves in the crevasses between their bodies.

Dalton pushed his fingers into the hair at the back of her neck. "I love you, Clarisse. I'm here now." He kissed her lips, held her tight and then walked her the rest of the way home.

25

A Meeting

They sat around the kitchen table after Clarisse had left, with Macy and McCann, to begin the inoculation of the people of Hope. "We have to discuss this with Lieutenant Harding. We can't sneak back across the border and capture a few terrorists, bring them here, and conduct medical experiments on them," Reuben said, shaking his head at their willingness to deceive the people of Hope.

"If we do what you're suggesting and tell them of our plans," Dalton said. "There's a good chance they'll try to stop us."

"If they do, we should move on and then conduct our mad plan elsewhere," Reuben said.

"That's just it, Reuben. She needs the lab here, and the facilities to keep them secure. She needs to be able to work on developing the virus, and we need the containment they have here for the test subjects." Dalton shook his head. "Yes, it's dirty work, but they've left us no choice. This is our only option. It's the only way we can defeat them without losing any more of our people. It's the only way, Reuben." He ended the argument with that statement, letting its intended finality sink in.

Reuben, who seemed at odds with the proposal from the start, let the words settle around them. He had no other answers, and Dalton knew this because he knew Reuben. The man who was moral to a fault; he never ignored an opportunity to put them in their place, to remind them that they were human and were thus held to a higher standard than were the animals who had landed them in this situation to begin with. Dalton could see that Reuben quarreled within himself. What more could he say to convince him this was their only option? Were they to lie down and die because of the needs of one group's corrupt religious ideals? That's what it boiled down to: world domination. No one lives but those with fanatic ideals.

"How are you going to keep this a secret from them?" Reuben finally asked. Appealing to Graham's common sense, he added, "Harding's people are going to find out. *Then* what?"

Dalton hung his head in defeat. He had hoped he'd put an end to any comeback but clearly he had not.

"He's right," Rick piped in.

Dalton was shocked. He'd never thought he'd hear Rick side with Reuben; that never happened.

"I say we tell them from the start," Rick said. "We're going to need their help."

"And how do you figure we go about doing that?"

"Look around, man. They have equipment, we don't. They have trucks, planes and all kinds of gear stored here."

"They don't use it," Reuben said. "They don't leave this place. I talked to one of the guards. They've been holed up here since before there was an official lockdown. These people are probably some of the only survivors left in Canada."

"And they won't even be *that* for long," Dalton added. "The terrorists will come here after they've finished transforming our homeland into their version of a religious state. They'll do the same thing here. If we tell the people of Hope what we're planning, they'll have to understand that this is in their best interest or they'll never go for it. They won't. I know their mentality. They'll refuse to help, and might even kick us out."

"Or arrest us again," Rick offered.

Dalton picked up his coffee and saluted Rick's last-minute suggestion. It was strange, staying in someone else's home. The three houses they occupied were fully furnished and well taken care of. They were offered several more, but the women wanted to keep everyone close together. They'd become dependent on one another for safety and were used to living side by side now. When separated, they felt anxious and vulnerable. Dalton suspected this was true of ancient people too; where there was danger they needed to cling to one another in greater numbers to survive. It meant that, if attacked, chances were that someone would survive.

The other guys around the table were quiet, each thinking of the consequences of this decision. "All right," Dalton said, "It's agreed that we will talk to the lieutenant about our plans in hopes that he agrees with it."

Graham startled Dalton and everyone else when he said, "Wait a second. I used to think the way this man does, I suspect." His friend looked troubled before he continued. "I don't think we should tell Harding all of it. You're right, Dalton, he won't be complicit in this plan. Let's leave out the genocide. Let's only tell him that we need the test subjects for questioning, to find out their motives. Clarisse can do the injections in secret. She's only going to need a few vials of blood, and then she'll need to infect them and wait to see what happens. Harding and his people won't know what's going on if we can get to the patients. Clarisse could say it's in our best interest to inoculate them against the China Flu as a disguise for the real purpose of infecting them."

"That's true," Rick agreed, "but how are we going to get to them? The guards will have control of them."

An idea came to Sam, and he reached for the map at the center of the table. He unfolded the map and laid it flat, scrutinizing the area. "We'll leave tomorrow and travel east on the main highway over to the nearest border crossing." He pointed to a likely spot. "Here. Sumas-Huntingdon Border Crossing. It's only an hour and a half away, and there's bound to be some of those jerks hanging around a border crossing; we can grab a few. We'll say we were out hunting and found them sneaking around. Clarisse is just now vaccinating these folks; they need two weeks before they're immune to the virus. We'll say *we* need to watch over them, so they don't get infected until they're immune. Y'know, it's the *least* we can do—since they've been so *hospitable* and all . . ." He finished in a slightly sarcastic tone that made them all laugh. Sam's humor came out at the oddest of times.

"So, then, we'll explain it to Harding as an opportunity for intel?" Graham asked.

"That's perfect," Rick said, and the others nodded.

26

A Hunting Trip

"Where did they head off to?" Lieutenant Harding asked again.

Clarisse crossed her legs casually but tried to contain her nervousness. "They're on a hunting trip for meat to process. You see, we lost much of our emergency reserves when we fled, and we can't expect you to feed us indefinitely."

Harding sat at his side of the desk, contemplating her reasoning. Your commander didn't mention this to me yesterday," he said, shuffling papers around.

"Yes, well . . . you see, he's not my commander, exactly. We work as a team."

"But, he has the final say in any argument, correct?"

"No, no he doesn't. Like I said, we're a team. We usually come to an agreement fairly easily. If there's a difference we weigh the options and go with the best decision."

Harding nodded at her with a slightly condescending smile, as if Clarisse were an innocent child. He obviously didn't agree with her group's methods, but they had worked well for them thus far.

She couldn't help but think that the longtime residents of Hope must feel like prisoners. They couldn't speak their mind. They might be allowed to leave, but it was the fact that they had to be *allowed to* in the first place that bothered Clarisse. She had to remember what freedom meant and how fleeting that concept could be from one place to another.

"I expect them to return by tomorrow night," she said. "There's nothing to worry about. We like to maintain our stores, and since you kept safe what we already had—and we really appreciate that, by the way—we won't have to do much more hunting. We'll share, if that's what might be bothering you. Do you want us to share our hunt, lieutenant?"

"Henry," he corrected her. "No, not at all. In fact, I had a meeting yesterday with our supply crew, and we talked about how to include another thirty people into our calculations. It's not a problem. We have gardens and farms within our borders. We work together and can maintain our way of life without having to leave here, and you don't put an extra burden on our supplies. What I'm saying is, it wasn't necessary to go on a hunt."

"Yes, I understand your point of view, but what you're not taking into account now is that since we are not vulnerable to the virus we're not threatened by the possible exposure. Perhaps we can trade some venison for beef or bacon," she said with a smile. "Soon your people will be able to go out hunting as well."

He sat up in his chair. He'd barely thought about it. "It's a foreign concept for us here. We're just getting used to the idea. We've maintained the borders all this time. I'm not sure how the townspeople will take to this new freedom. It's probably best to start off on small trips."

"Yes, I think Dalton would be happy to take a small group out at a time, show them the ropes. Of course, we all also have the danger of the terrorists out there. Right now that's the biggest threat. I wish you'd heed our words and prepare better."

Harding held up his hand. "Yes, yes, I know what you're going to say. Dalton and I had an extensive conversation about this too." He picked up his pencil and began tapping it on the desk. "I concede that they're a threat—but not an immediate one, as far as I can see. You have time here to regroup, to plan, but there's no way you'd have had the time to figure out how to exterminate them from your own country."

Clarisse squirmed in her seat a little when he used the term *exterminate*.

"I encouraged Dalton to consider joining us here. Our borders are secure, as you can see. We have an elaborate setup, and it's sustainable. Our people are happy for the most part. They've recovered from the shock of the pandemic. And now, thanks to you, they're also immune to the very threat that killed so many."

Clarisse thought he was reaching a bit, but she said nothing.

"Not that I'm trying to argue with you, Henry, but your people are depressed; they're *not* thriving. They wake up each day wondering if hiding here was the right thing to do instead of dying with the rest of humanity. They're not happy, they're barely surviving. They're not free to leave these boundaries you've kept them in. Don't get me wrong. It's all warranted—you've saved their lives, after all—but they're not happy. And honestly, neither are we. We've survived, but we've lost a lot in the process. *Happy* is not something any of us will be for a very long time. That's a luxury for the future—*if* we survive this. *If* we make it beyond the terror."

Harding wasn't going to argue with her either. "Well, yes, you're right there. I hope you consider staying with us here. If not, I'd advise you to travel farther north instead of south. Going back will be nothing short of suicide if what you say is true."

"It's a fact, actually. They'll come here eventually."

Harding looked a bit uncomfortable with her last statement and twisted sideways in his chair. He glanced at Clarisse a few times before saying, "So, have you located your dogs yet?"

He's changing the subject.

"No, we haven't, and the kids are becoming more restless. We don't want them traveling farther out, so we've decided they need to give up the search."

"You're team seems quite attached to those dogs."

"Yes, well, one, in particular, is very special to part of the group. His name is Sheriff, and he's saved lives. He's one of us. It's going to be a big loss if we don't eventually find him."

Harding leaned back in his chair. "We've had a few dogs here in Hope—still do. Our rule was, if they showed aggression at all, they had to be put down. That led to a near extinction of our pets. One neighbor would turn in another and, well, after a while, even the tame dogs nearly disappeared. Only a few old-timers are still around. All of them are out of breeding range. Before we realized what was happening, they were all but gone.

"The cats, on the other hand, began to breed out of control, and we put them down because they were beginning to cause quite a problem. There are a lot of lessons living in a closed society that life on the other side doesn't teach you. One of those things is when to recognize a bad idea in a vacuum. It's not so easy when you think as a collective rather than an individual. So now we have few pets and those we do have are not fertile. They're harbingers of a time past and they're loved but, like an endangered species, they're fleeting. Because of a few bad decisions, our lone society suffers the lack of furry companionship."

Clarisse couldn't help but wonder if he was talking about more than just their pet situation. She'd already noticed the lack of newborns among the residents of Hope. Perhaps after they were vaccinated, they might have dreams for a future and therefore look toward having children again. Even the young teens she ran into looked downcast and unsociable with one another, preferring to linger with their parents rather than one another. Macy had tried on more than one occasion to interact with some of the girls her age, but every attempt had been met with one-word answers to her questions.

"Well, if we can find the dogs perhaps we can have a breeding program. Sheriff and Frank are both males, but Elsa is a female. Sheriff isn't fixed; he was a police dog, and they don't neuter them in order to keep a certain level of aggression—for obvious reasons. The female, Elsa—I'm not certain, but I don't believe she's been spayed. Perhaps we'll have a litter of puppies and can reintroduce dogs to Hope. There are few mistakes a society can make that can't be undone, this may be one of them. Forgive me for saying so, but I've noticed there are no young children or pregnant women here. I completely understand why people are holding back, but now that they're inoculated, perhaps some will consider having babies." She smiled at him and stood. "And speaking of children, I do need to return and check on my own group. I'd noticed that Tala is walking a little slower these days and I need to examine her."

"How long before she delivers?"

"Only a few weeks now. We're all very excited."

"Do you need to use the medical facilities here?"

"That's a good question. I've never actually delivered a baby before. I've attended live births, but I've never delivered one myself so this will be new to me. Do you have any midwives?"

Harding looked dumbstruck. "I don't know. That's a very good question. I'll ask around. We obviously haven't had any need for one before this."

Clarisse laughed slightly at his composure. "Well, thank you once again."

He held her hand a second longer than necessary. "Clarisse, we can't thank you enough. If there's anything you need, don't hesitate to ask."

She smiled and hoped he continued to feel that way when he eventually found out about their plan. "Well, have a good evening," she said and walked outside of his office and back to the path that led her to their side of town.

It was a sunny late spring afternoon, without even the need for a sweater. As Clarisse walked she thought it odd that there were cars parked along the houses and in driveways, yet no one drove anywhere; they always walked. There probably wasn't gasoline left in their tanks, but in the grand scheme of things that didn't matter: no one was leaving Hope. The cars and trucks remained solely as a reminder of what used to be. Perhaps in the early days they had been a reminder that the townspeople couldn't leave even if they wanted to. And, since then, maybe the vehicles had become invisible to them, like nothing more than a potted plant in front of a house.

27

The Candidates

The light, just after the darkest hour of early morning, gave little visibility as they crept along Highway 3, first west and then south across the US border. Dalton figured they'd likely encounter a few scouting groups like the one they'd run into when he was mauled by the bear. They'd left the day before, and as they drove through the guard post in Hope he'd explained they were going hunting. It wasn't a complete falsehood; a slight deception, but not exactly a lie.

Their first task had been, in fact, to do some deer hunting closer to Hope. Sam had sat out a few traps the previous afternoon, and after checking the first few they thought it might take them longer to actually come up with a deer to show for their efforts. But when they came upon the last trap, lo and behold, a nice buck stood, tethered. Sam hated to do it this way, said it was cheating and dishonest. Dalton felt for him and was about to offer to do the deed himself when Sam pulled back an arrow and cleanly shot the deer.

Once across the border, it took almost no time to locate the first jihadists—too little time, and that fact made the men nervous. The terrorists had moved north already; their vehicles were parked all over the roadway, so it was safe to assume they were camped nearby. Several miles away from their approach, the men stopped and put on their equipment. The plan was simple enough: grab three of the jihadists without making a sound or getting anyone killed, then hightail it back to Hope.

This was a dangerous mission, and it took five of them to do it. Graham, the father to be, was back in Hope, left to care for everyone —especially Tala.

Dalton still worried about McCann after the last failed mission. It had been too much too soon, an early and intense introduction to war for the young man. McCann was capable, but he had a strong survival trait running through him. Dalton worried that even if they succeeded, McCann would harden. He'd seen it happen to so many others before, and maybe it was a necessary fact of wartime, but Dalton didn't want to see it happen to the young man. McCann was the strongest leader they had of the next generation. Mark was a great kid, but McCann would be the one to make sure they all survived, that Dalton's sons would grow up to live a full life.

The next generation had been on his mind a lot lately with the coming of Tala's child. They needed to vanquish these intruders, take their own country back, and work toward building their future.

After they had hiked in silence for two miles to avoid detection, Rick spotted a likely candidate.

The guy wasn't much more than a kid himself—younger, even than McCann's twenty years. Dressed in a white headscarf and robe, he stood stoically beside a line of vehicles in the dark. Perhaps he was the night watch? The young man looked bored with the task; he leaned against the vehicle, his head lolling to one side as he fought off sleep.

Dalton and Rick made hand signals to each other after locating the vacant tents of the others in the group who were apparently out for the night. Knowing there were probably two or three more night guards on watch, they made their way around the area to give them a wide berth. After recognizing three individuals left on watch on the perimeter, they decided this would be the least invasive way to go: just capture the guards and quietly make their way back across the border.

They devised a plan and split into two groups, Dalton, Sam and McCann in one, Rick and Reuben in the other. This ensured a sound set of skills for each group as they scoped the perimeter. Dalton's group eyed the potential medical experiment candidate and planned to approach him from behind the vehicle. As the young man leaned left against the side of the truck with his hand near the trigger of his gun, Dalton approached from the right and silently looped his arm around the victim's neck, applying quick and continuous pressure to his carotid artery; Sam grabbed the guard's rifle. McCann injected the guy with a vial of the anesthetic Propofol, which rendered him unconscious.

Sam handed the rifle to McCann and looped the candidate over his shoulders in a fireman's carry. Dalton guarded Sam as they retreated to their vehicles, quickly followed by Reuben, who carried his own contender, apparently also captured without a sound and in much the same way.

Rick and McCann silently scanned the area. They needed one more nominee for the sake of "research," and they knew he was waiting nearby, oblivious to their antics.

They snuck off toward the third guy on watch and found him to be larger, older, and wide awake, moving right and then left, three or four paces at a time. This guy had more experience and was probably the leader of the three. Rick shook his head at Dalton. Pretty soon the alert guy would realize his other minions were out of commission and would come looking for them.

Dalton scanned the campsite again, and realized the lumps on the ground were a few tentless terrorists sleeping not ten yards away. Getting to this guy and taking him down to sleepy land wasn't going to be easy without alerting these lumps.

Rick made a few hand signals suggesting that they time it right and run up behind him. The problem was, they were out in the open, and it would only take any small sound to alert those sleeping.

They could wait until an opportunity arose, but that wasn't going to work out either. Finally, Rick noticed that McCann was trying to get his attention, but since he lacked a proper knowledge of hand signals he was becoming more and more frustrated.

Dalton gave him his attention. McCann pointed at the walking guy and shook his head; then pointed at one of the sleeping lumps instead. Dalton dipped his head. *Why didn't I think of that?*

Bypassing the lone guard, they ninja-crept their way to the other end of the group and located the first lump that was farthest from the rest on the outside perimeter.

A blanket covered the form, and as Dalton grabbed at the face and neck to subdue any noise, Rick went for the arms. Once the form stopped struggling, they carried the body away through the night. Halfway to the waiting truck, Dalton stopped and exposed an arm for McCann to administer the Propofol. But when he pulled away the fabric, they were shocked to find out they had a woman in their arms. Dalton had assumed they'd snagged another young man; he never considered that they might actually have a woman in their scouting party.

Dalton met eyes with the others to see if there were any objections. No one said a word. McCann went ahead and plunged in the needle to put her to sleep. They had no idea what her story might be; it was a mystery for now, and besides that, it was too late to turn back.

Once their three prisoners were inside the vehicle, Reuben drove back through the night. The short drive back to camp—only about an hour and a half—caused all of them to realize that this spreading jihadist disease had come far too close. Sam had cuffed the prisoners' hands and legs together and applied duct tape to their mouths.

"How long will they stay out?" Rick asked.

McCann answered, "forty-five minutes to an hour, depending on their weight. The woman, she'll be out for longer."

"Woman?" Reuben said.

"Ah, yeah. Looks like the last one we got was a woman, though we didn't know it at the time."

Sam pulled back the cover, revealing the woman's headscarf. He patted her down for weapons, and when his hand roamed over something solid, he found she had a nine-millimeter Russian Makarov tucked into her waistband. He held it up for the others to see in the dim light.

"Well, she's not a prisoner, clearly," Rick commented.

"Guess we'll find out later when she wakes up."

Sam handed the gun to Rick and searched for other weapons; there was a knife strapped to her right inner thigh and another smaller one strapped to her inner left ankle.

"Christ, man, check her again just in case you missed something," Rick said as Sam handed him the knives.

Sam found another blade under her arm, tucked into the bindings around her chest. Now, fairly confident that she was unarmed, they pulled her wrists together and cuffed them securely. "She looks to be mid- to late twenties. Maybe Arabic, but who knows?" Sam said

"Find anything on the others?" Dalton asked.

Sam chuckled, and Reuben laughed out loud. Pointing to the unconscious man on the right side of the vehicle, Sam said "Oh, yeah! This guy not only had a rifle but also this damn big knife and this pistol. The kid had the rifle he had on him as well as this little curved knife."

"Hey, give me that," Dalton said. Sam handed him the small knife. After examining it, Dalton asked, "You know what this is?"

They all gave him a blank look and a silence to fill. "It's a kirpan, a Sikh baptismal knife. It's ceremonial. Does he have a comb or a bracelet on him?"

"No, I didn't find one," Sam said, "but that was tucked inside of his boot."

"You think he's a Sikh?" Reuben asked while he kept his eyes on the road.

"I don't know what to think. He could have picked it off a victim. Who knows? Nothing sacred belongs to one man anymore. They've ruined it all. Just like the Holocaust, only on a ghastly scale, if that's even possible. We're on the brink of extinction here because of them. Don't feel sorry for them—not one bit." Dalton eyed McCann and then the others. They had a woman, a young man, and another man, and they were all the enemy. They were mere people, yet they were monsters who had taken many lives; theirs was a selfishness that extended to all things, even a multitude of souls.

28

Trouble at the Border

Graham covered the front of the lonely house while Mark guarded the back. They didn't need to keep up such tight security, but knowing the others were out hunting for the enemy, Graham wanted to keep an eye open.

He sent Tala off to bed after Clarisse had given them a heart-to-heart talk about the baby's impending birth. Clarisse had examined her and said she might come into labor soon; it was both a thrilling and scary prospect, but Graham was more scared than thrilled.

The question remained as to what happened with the virus in a newborn's system. They just didn't know, and Tala would have little time to intervene if the virus took hold. Quarantine would be implemented right away, and Clarisse hinted at the severity of such an action. She warned them that since they both carried the virus, she would immediately put the baby into isolation once it was born.

Graham still didn't understand. What difference would it make if he and Tala held the baby after it was born? He would do whatever Clarisse insisted upon, but if the infant could not even be held by its mother after birth, what chance would it have at long-term survival? This scenario is what he had feared from the very beginning.

It was a frustrating dilemma, but Clarisse insisted that the baby be placed immediately into a quarantined incubator in the lab. That way the environment could be controlled. She would draw blood right away and begin testing the infant's immune system for antibodies. With any luck they would be present, and all fears for the next generation would fall away.

Suddenly Graham heard a commotion down the road. Headlights beamed at the main gate, and Graham told Mark to hang tight while he went to check it out.

The headlights beamed through the thick, moist air, and Graham heard shuffling as he made his way to the gate. Loud voices rang out, and instead of his usual fast walk, with its customary limp, Graham picked up the pace to a skipping kind of jog. He didn't want anyone to get hurt; these plans were risky, and making sure everyone came out of this alive and uninjured was his most pressing concern. As he neared the gate, voices became more earnest and insistent.

"You need to stay back!" Rick yelled.

"Why? What are you hiding?" one of the guards yelled.

Dalton made eye contact with Graham as he approached and nodded his head, indicating that they had been successful. At least that's what Graham took the gesture to mean.

Dalton then focused on the guards. "We were attacked by a few terrorists on our way in. We captured them, but I'm sure they're carriers. You guys have only had the vaccine within your systems for a few days. Someone get Clarisse over here. She'll be able to tell us more."

"I'm calling the lieutenant," a guard said, still not believing them.

"Yes, please do. Ask him if we can put them in quarantine. I think that's the best thing to do here. I don't want any of you exposed, so please"—he waved them away—"keep your distance. Graham, can you get Clarisse?"

"Sure. I'll be right back." Graham jogged away from the scene knowing the game was on. The first phase in the battle to regain their country had now begun.

29

A Resolution

"It's a problem," Harding said to Clarisse, Dalton, and Graham, who were seated in his office.

"It's *not* a problem," said Clarisse. We can keep them in quarantine and then try to get as much information out of them as possible."

"They're too close to us," Dalton warned.

"That's right, Dalton. They're too close now that *you've brought them here*," Graham said, feigning anger. "I have a wife and unborn child to protect, dammit!"

"I agree with Graham," Harding said. "I don't see how we can gain any knowledge just having them here without the risk of exposure and leaving a trail for others to follow."

"This is an opportunity to learn from them. We have three of them. I can run some tests to see how they're immune to the virus. They must have developed their own vaccine," Clarisse implored.

"At the same time, I can try to get as much information about their plans and hopefully we can stay ahead of them instead of waiting here like sitting ducks," Dalton added.

"I can see how that's appealing," said Harding as he leaned back in his chair, thinking. "But let's consider the risks. My people are still vulnerable. Graham's child will be born any day now, and that makes you vulnerable as well.

"We can maintain them in the quarantine buildings," Dalton offered. My people will care for them so there's no exposure to the citizens of Hope. We can do this. We have the skills and expertise."

"I won't allow any torture techniques," Harding said, suddenly sitting up in his chair and grabbing his pencil. Graham could tell he was considering their proposal.

"Just so we're clear, how do you define *torture* here?" Dalton asked.

"No waterboarding. No pain infliction of any kind. No starvation. Nothing inhumane."

Dalton shook his head. "Do you even know what waterboarding entails?"

"Yes, of course I do, and I won't relent on this, Dalton."

"It doesn't matter what they've done, their inhumane treatment of our people? You still insist they be treated as humans?" Dalton asked.

"I do. No matter what they've done. I insist they be treated like humans because we're humane. If we lose that, we're no better than they are."

That statement drove home to Graham that their decision to keep their real plans a secret was a good one. Had they come out with their true intentions, they'd have had no hope at all.

Tap, tap, tap . . . Harding's pencil eraser against the desk filled the silence. Both men were thinking, but one was played in the other's hand unwittingly.

"Deal," Dalton said with reluctance.

Now it was Graham's turn to once again act out of step with the others. "*What*? How can you guarantee they won't expose everyone, including Tala and the baby? Clarisse will have to bring Tala into the medical facilities when she goes into labor."

"No, I can set up shop in the house. I'll bring all the equipment there. Tala will have no need to return to the medical building," she said.

Harding looked at him with a sympathetic expression. "I understand your concern, Graham, but I have faith in Clarisse's abilities. I'm sure she'll take all the necessary precautions."

Something had just transpired without words between Dalton and Graham. Dalton couldn't really put his finger on it, but having Harding defend Clarisse with praise put him on edge suddenly. He cleared his throat loudly.

"Yeah, well. We, all know how capable Clarisse is. That's not a problem," Dalton said. Graham saw Clarisse nudge Dalton in the leg with her boot, but Harding missed it.

"Yes. Problem solved then, right?" Harding spoke in a tone that indicated the issue was resolved, and all rose from their seats.

"Let's hope we don't regret this," Graham said as he shook hands with Harding and the others.

Once they left the building Graham let the other two walk ahead of him while he strolled back with his hands in his pockets and head dropped in thought. He supposed he'd put on a good act, but to some degree he truly was worried about the effects of their plan—not only for his child but for them all. Part of him wanted to take his group farther north and forget all of this. Though he hadn't talked about it with anyone, he was sure McCann would do it. He didn't want to split up the group, but with this coming conflict, fleeing north was tempting, and he decided to keep the possibility open. It would certainly mean their survival in the short term, but for how long could they outrun the terrorists? Would there ever be a future for their children if they didn't take a stand now? And if *they* didn't stand up, who would?

30

Interrogation

"Allahu Akbar!" the young terrorist yelled at Rick while nearly foaming at the mouth after an extensive one-sided questioning session.

"Yeah? Back at ya, jerk," Rick said as he got up and left in disgust from the interrogation room.

Dalton had insisted that they were maintained in separate holding cells, and while they were still unconscious, Clarisse had withdrawn several vials of blood from each candidate to begin her testing.

Rick washed his hands in the quarantine partition before leaving the room under guard supervision.

"You guys should keep your distance from here," Rick warned them.

"We're under orders to make sure you don't torture the captives," the guard said.

Rick faced him squarely. He couldn't believe this was still an issue. "Look, that's not going to happen. We gave our word. You can put up cameras if you'd like. Hell, I'll set them up for you. I simply don't want you exposed to them. I don't want there to be any more deaths from this damn virus. Don't you get that?"

The Tyvek-suited guard watched him silently while he dried his hands on the towel. "I understand, sir. I'm just following orders."

Rick nodded. "I'll talk to Harding. He's taking too many chances with your lives. Keep that in mind when you take orders from him."

"We're all living on borrowed time, sir."

Rick scoffed. "With that attitude, you won't be around for long. Fight for it, soldier. It's you or them. Get that through your head now. We are individuals, no longer a collective."

The young guard nodded but stayed silent. Rick had ulterior motives in keeping the guards at a distance, but at the same time, he and the others noticed how it seemed the citizens of Hope showed little hope within themselves.

After weeks of living with them, he'd observed that they seemed resigned to an eventual death and that perhaps only a time and circumstance kept them from that fine line. They had no motivation to live, no survival instinct left. They were cared for night and day by rules created by their leaders. There was no living; there was only routine until they decided it wasn't worth it, and most of the citizens lived in that fog. Suicide was common.

The arrival of the Americans had sparked one or more to delay their own deaths through mild curiosity alone. After looking at their lives and the way they lived here, Rick realized there were some lives not worth living. They needed to wake up, or they would easily be defeated when the terrorists arrived. The town residents seemed to willingly welcome defeat. Hope would no longer exist in either name or worth if they allowed this to continue.

Rick passed the guard and rounded the corner to Dalton's new office.

"Anything?" Dalton asked.

"Nah, same crap, different desert."

"Well, we still have the woman to question, and then we'll step it up. We're looking for names and mission goals. Locations, et cetera. And, of course, if they have large numbers of any major weapons."

Rick nodded, then lowered his voice so no passing guard could hear them. "What about Clarisse? How long did she say it would take to develop this virus?"

Dalton shook his head. "It depends, of course. First, she has to locate the antibodies and then isolate probable markers. Define how it's different from the ones we carry and then reverse-engineer the vaccine to create a virus that will in turn attack them with lethal precision." He faced Rick with a pained expression. "It could take months or she might be successful next week. We're in it for the long haul, probably. We just have to come up with a list of probable excuses to keep this on the down-low."

"Let's start with creating some distance between the guards and us. It's no joke that they take quarantine lightly, and what we don't need is for one of them to come down with the virus. These people are almost begging for death. They're nearly zombies. We need to get Harding to understand that they're taking unnecessary risks."

"Yeah, you're right. Having them inside the building is too much of a risk. I'll swing by there and have a chat with him and check in on Clarisse at the same time."

"Okay, I'll hold down the fort and post the guards outside the building while I'm at it. I told them I'd even set up cameras in the interrogation rooms for their monitoring needs, if that's what it took to keep them from exposure."

"Hmmm," Dalton said as he exited.

Rick had a feeling Dalton was checking on Clarisse this often for more than one reason. He himself had caught the vibe coming from the lieutenant toward their esteemed doctor, and he was sure it was something that Dalton wouldn't take lightly. He knew Clarisse could handle herself, but if there was an infatuation there, Dalton's head wouldn't be in the game as much as he should be. And they needed him at his best for this.

Rick sat in Dalton's chair, leaned back into his best thinking position, and tapped the bald spot on his head. Deep in thought, he wondered how his suspicions could be used to their advantage. Then he remembered who they were directed toward and reprimanded himself. Clarisse would never go along with something like that . . . unless it was her idea to begin with.

31

Control

"They're taking the necessary precautions," Harding said after Dalton explained his concern.

"I'm not sure they are. You see, the reason this virus spread so rapidly is because it can remain alive in air vapor for over an hour after an occupant leaves a room. Please don't take risks like this. Look, in two weeks you'll be immune to the virus and I won't beg this of you. But for now please station them outside the building."

Harding's pencil was in his hand, and Dalton wanted nothing more than to rip it from him if he started bouncing the blasted eraser against the desk again.

Harding took a deep breath, glancing at Dalton and then looking back down at his desk. "All right, I'll call them back. You're putting me in a position of forced trust. You know that, right? I have no choice, and the lives of my people depend on your convictions."

Dalton nodded. "I understand your hesitation. All I can say is, if it were my men, I'd do the same. Your people need something to hope for. It's ironic, the town's name. You need to give them something, Henry. Anything to hold onto for the future."

"You've already done that. You gave them the cure. It came with bad news of an imminent attack by the terrorists, but yes, you've given them more hope than I was ever able to."

"It should never have gotten so bad, Henry. What the hell were you guys thinking? Yes, you saved them by acting quickly, but you have to give them something to look forward to too. They can't just stagnate here without anything to show for it except a breath. If we had not entered your world, you'd still have needless suicides."

"No. No, we wouldn't. It was our previous leader. Complete isolation was his rule. We argued about his methods, but he wouldn't budge. He was a brilliant man, but a depressed one. He killed himself sitting right here. Right after I had had an argument with him because of his rigid rules. Ed was my friend. He couldn't live with the knowledge that he was wrong. In the end, it was his pride that killed him."

"He wasn't completely wrong, Henry. He did keep all of you alive, but at what cost? Human beings cannot live without hope for a future. If there's no hope, there's nothing to look forward to. And then what good is life?"

The pensive look on Harding's face granted his agreement.

"Let's work on this together," Dalton continued. "As dumb as it sounds, right now we're on the losing side of the human race. They, the terrorists, don't deserve the term. We're in this together, and we must find a way to triumph over them."

"Of course. Why don't we have some of your men train with mine? At least they would feel less vulnerable. Actually, some of our guards also need better training. Though they can hold their own, I do believe yours have some tricks to share with them. And I'd like to have Clarisse train a member or two of our group in medical care."

"I'm sure she'd be honored to. She's already working on two trainees in our group." Dalton knew it was coming, but he'd let Harding take his time. A silence hung in the air. He faced the window where all the spring petals from a cherry tree had long blown away, leaving only the dark red foliage as its showcase until it bore fruit once again.

"She's *with* you, I take it?" Harding asked without making eye contact.

Dalton didn't answer right away. He wanted a deep impression to remain when he said the words. "She's more than my own life. She's mine, Henry . . . and I am hers."

Harding eventually met his stern expression. He smiled with resignation and said, "You're a lucky man, but then that's an extreme understatement where Clarisse is concerned."

"Yes, it is. Speaking of whom, I'll go and check in on her now." He stood from his chair and shook Harding's hand.

"I think we should often meet and discuss our progress," Harding said.

"Yeah, that's a good idea. I'll keep you posted on the harmless interrogations. So far there's been nothing of value."

"They attacked your hunting team, you said?" Harding asked again with a hint of suspicion.

"Yes, they came up behind us. We were silent hunting, and I turned my head at the right moment and saw the young man behind a tree. Rick circled around with Reuben and McCann. Sam and I found the woman hidden nearby. By the time we were through, we had three. We didn't detect any others with them, but we could be wrong. Do you have anyone here who speaks Arabic?"

"No, I don't believe so."

Rick and Reuben both know a few words, and they're asking most of the questions. So far, the only thing they're spouting is religious chants. I'm sure you can imagine," Dalton said.

Harding laughed. "Of course, what else would they do? They're probably so brainwashed by now, they weren't expecting to find anyone who'd fight back . . ." His voice trailed off, and Dalton wondered if Harding had been struck with a moment of terror. "They could have made it here, and they would have found a whole society of people who wouldn't fight back. They would have been correct in their assumptions then."

"They didn't, Henry, and they won't. We're here now, and we will fight with you."

Harding, drained of all color, sat back down and nodded his head in solemn restraint.

"See you later, Henry," Dalton exited, leaving Harding to deal with the thought of what their policies had nearly cost them.

After a short walk, Dalton came to Clarisse's door, where a guard waved him in without a word. He found her, as he had so many times before, dressed in a white lab coat. He wasn't sure where she kept finding those things; they always looked as if they had come directly from the dry cleaners. She sat on a high black stool, teetering over a microscope.

"Hi Dalton," she said without looking up.

"How do you do that? How'd you know it was me?"

"I can always tell it's you," she said, still not looking up.

"How? By smell?" Dalton crept up on her back.

"No, I just know, that's all."

When he reached her, he couldn't resist looping his arms around her waist. After his conversation with Harding, he needed to hold her, to claim her—mainly to reassure himself that she was still his.

"Just a second," she said and placed one of her hands on her waist over his hand where he held her.

Dalton waited silently, smelling her hair, twisted and flattened into a bun at the back of her head. He trailed little kisses from behind her left ear down the back of her neck.

She scrunched up her shoulders. "*Dal-ton*. I'm trying to work here."

"Sorry. I need you," he confessed.

"I can't. Not now, at least. Later," she said, shooting him a devilish smile.

"Ohh-kay," he relented, hugging her tightly against him. He swallowed hard and decided to play nice and ask her about the progress. "So, any news?"

She swallowed and shook her head. "Not yet. The antibodies are much different from the ones we created. It's going to take some work. Undistracted work . . . so that I can come up with something."

He knew what she meant by *something*. It pained him to have such a horrible task weighing on her conscious. He put his hands on her shoulders and massaged her neck by placing his thumbs on the two long muscles flanking her spine. "Hang in there. I know you'll find a way."

32

Missing Sheriff

McCann awoke in a cloudy haze. A noise crept into his subconscious, waking far too early, and it wasn't the little boy snoring lightly on the twin bed next to his. He quietly eased himself off his bed, careful not to step too hard on the squeaky floorboards lest he wake Bang. He grabbed his jeans from the foot of his bed and slipped them on, then ran his fingers through his hair, leaving it spiky.

He padded barefoot across the room and down the darkened hall-way, stopping at Marcy and Macy's door and tapping lightly with his knuckles. The door opened, and Macy's red-rimmed eyes stared back at him.

"What is it?" she asked. She turned away, leaving the door open. McCann walked in and closed it behind him. The first thing he noticed was that Marcy wasn't in the bed she usually shared with her twin.

"Where's your sister?"

"She's next door. Olivia has an extra room, and Marcy wanted her own."

McCann nodded, filing away the information and knowing that Mark, too, had opted to stay next door. He'd talk to Mark later.

"Why are you upset?"

Macy sat on her bed and shot him a flicker of rage. "You *know* why. I can't find him."

McCann leaned with his back against the door. He could tell she'd barely slept, and he guessed she'd been out most of the night searching for the dogs. She was probably leaving food out for them again, even though he'd warned her that that would only attract deer and bears.

"We've seen signs of them, but they're smart, Macy. Sheriff's no ordinary dog. I'm sure he'll show up eventually. You can't beat yourself up over this."

"He saved my life. I can't just forget him."

"No one is asking you to, Macy. I'll go out on horseback and search for him today; I don't think Clarisse needs my help in the lab. Do you want to come with me?"

Macy nodded. Her lips trembled, and tears flooded her eyes, spilling down her cheeks. McCann crossed the room, taking her into his arms, desperate to relieve the pain in her heart.

"Macy, we will find him," he promised, shaking her with conviction.

"I can't lose Sheriff, too, McCann. My parents . . . Ennis. I . . . I *need* him."

"I know," he whispered. "I'm sure he's waiting for us. He's watching and waiting until it's safe to come out. He's a part of us Macy. He'll show up."

"What if . . . what if he didn't make it?"

McCann pulled her harder against his chest. "He *did*. Don't even think it. Don't give that a chance to come true." And before she could protest he pressed his lips to hers and kissed her. Sliding his hand into the curls of her golden hair, he briefly allowed them both to escape the pain of loss and instead fuse a promise toward something they both possessed—hope.

33

A Birth

With Bang and Addy's help, Tala hung clean wet shirts on the line. She was grateful for the assistance, but couldn't help noticing how she never seemed to be able to get a moment alone; someone always hung in her shadow. Bang confided that Graham had asked him to keep an eye on her, and she couldn't blame Graham for his overprotective nature. She was so huge she couldn't even see her own feet. Graham's shirts had long become too tight around her midsection, and now she opted for the plus-size blouses she had found in the dresser of the house they were staying in.

It was odd, how she had once had a problem with using other people's belongings, the lingering smell of the departed still clinging to each fiber, but it no longer bothered her. Someone had once chosen this shirt from a department store for its attributes, be it a certain color, style or price. Now Tala wore it simply because it fit her swollen belly; she had no regard for whatever emotional value was once attached to it.

The early afternoon was warm already. Mark and Marcy were hunting, and Macy and McCann had gone in search of Sheriff again; a lost cause, Tala now thought. Most of the men were dealing with the prisoners, which left her alone in their house with the younger children. She had thought that washing the laundry and hanging it out to dry would help ease her feeling of confinement. With the two children at her heels, she washed a few loads and then let the kids struggle with the basket of wet clothes ready to hang on the line.

She snapped garment after garment in the air to rid them of wrinkles before clipping them to the line in the warm sun, while Bang and Addy chased one another through the tunnels the drying clothes provided. The damp clothing felt cool against Tala's arms, and the sun warmed her shoulders and back.

We could be happy here, she thought. Addy squealed with delight when Bang found her hiding place. The two had become inseparable, and Tala had at one point had to talk to Bang about doing too much for Addy, reminding him that she needed to learn to deal with life without hearing and how to do things for herself.

Tala reached into the basket for the next item but found it empty. She picked up the empty basket and headed toward the back door of the house. When she turned, a sudden need to scream loudly hit her even before she registered the pain. The children ran to her side. Olivia came running from next door as well.

Tala clasped Bang's small arm and yelled, "Get Graham."

Bang fled instantly without looking back. Olivia arrived at her side and helped her up. "The baby's coming!" Tala cried.

"I heard!" Olivia answered. Addy tugged on Tala's arm and pointed toward the house. "Yes, let's get you inside before you have another contraction. Is Clarisse coming? I've never delivered a baby before and I don't want to start now," Olivia said.

"I don't think I can move. I've got to push," Tala said straining with the sudden jolt of pain.

"No. Don't do that. I can't deliver . . . I was asleep when Bethany was born. No, no, no, you need to wait for Clarisse," she stammered.

Addy, very serious, tugged on Tala's arm again and then signed, *Let's get into the house.*

"Yes, okay," Tala said, and Olivia helped her get into a standing position. With the others holding Tala up they slowly made their way to the porch railing.

The pain hit her again. "Ahhhh!" Tala yelled, doubling over as if some outward force had slammed into her. "I can't!" she yelled.

There were four steps to climb, but Tala thought they might as well have been Mount Rainer because she couldn't attempt an assent of any kind.

The wave of pain passed after what seemed an eternity, leaving a wet sensation spreading beneath her legs and a compulsion to push like she'd never experienced before.

"Oh my God, it's coming!" Tala yelled.

"Nuh-uh! No!" Olivia yelled and tugged Tala toward the porch, willing her to take a step. "You wait. Wait for Clarisse!"

Tala knew that was an impossible request when another pain wave began. There was no stopping this. It was happening *here,* and it was happening *now.* A steady calm overcame her with the mounting urgency to push as the contraction crested the wave. Her eyes met Addy's. She could hear Olivia talking but tuned out the words. Tala released the railing after the pain subsided and signed for Addy to retrieve a blanket and pillow from the couch. The little girl ran through the door and quickly returned.

As Addy spread the blanket on the grass, Olivia frantically implored Tala to move into the house.

Another wave was beginning as Tala lay down on the blanket in the shade of the house and Addy helped her remove her wet shorts and underwear. Olivia reluctantly knelt beside Tala and held her hand. "I don't know what to do!" she cried.

Addy signed to her to get more blankets, and Olivia released Tala's hand and ran into the house. Tala lifted herself onto her elbows and strained against the pain. Olivia screamed Graham's name inside the house, but Tala barely registered it, so absorbed was she in the pain of her labor. With Addy kneeling by her side, she mounted the crest of another pain wave, screaming. Then, suddenly, Graham appeared at her side.

"I'm here. I'm here, and Clarisse is on the way," he said.

"The baby's coming *now*," she said with an urgency no one could ignore.

Graham smiled down at her with a silly grin. "Yes, I can see that; you're not usually outside half naked." He leaned over her to look below and said nervously, "The head's almost out."

Clarisse arrived, and everything happened in a rush of urgent voices and commands. Soon the sound of an infant, alive and wailing, filled the air, and others rushed to the backyard. "Everyone back," Clarisse screamed, angry as a bear, as she held the child tightly. "Graham, you've got to go to my office. *Now*. Get the incubator. Graham, now! *Go!*"

Rick arrived with the incubator before Graham had even crossed the road, and together they brought it to Clarisse.

"Put it down and back away. Both of you," Clarisse demanded, quickly taking the child to the machine after cutting away the umbilical cord.

Graham then went back to Tala's side. She was shaking and her teeth chattered. Blood and fluid covered everything, and someone handed him a blanket, which he wrapped around her.

"Is the baby okay? Is it a boy, or a girl?" Tala asked him with wild eyes.

It suddenly occurred to Graham that he didn't know the answer to either question. Clarisse hovered over the incubator and Dalton helped her carry the contraption into the house and to the designated room where they intended to keep the baby under surveillance. They spoke in hushed tones. The infant's cries echoed in the plastic box. Soon they seemed far away, and Graham was torn between rushing to the baby or remaining at Tala's side.

McCann and Macy arrived on horseback, having rushed back

from the woods after hearing Tala's screams. McCann flung himself from the mount and rushed to Graham and Tala.

"She's still bleeding," Graham said to McCann.

"Where's Clarisse?" McCann asked.

"With the baby."

"Let's get her inside." They wrapped Tala more tightly in the fresh blanket and carried her into the house and to their bedroom.

Tala heard the muffled tones of the baby crying. She closed her eyes and relished in the sound. "Is the baby okay?" she asked again.

Leaving McCann at Tala's side, he said "I'm going to find out. I'll be right back."

Entering the hallway, Graham found Sam standing in front of the closed bedroom door. Sam placed his hand on Graham's shoulder and shook his head. "You can't go in there, Graham. Just hang on. I'll tell you as soon as I know anything."

The baby continued a steady cadence of wails; it tore at Graham's soul. That was his child in there, his and Tala's, and he was being kept away.

"I don't . . . I don't even know if it's a boy or a girl. Can't you tell them, we need to see it, even for a moment?"

"It's for the child's own good, Graham," Sam answered. "If it catches the virus now, it may not survive. You have to understand that."

Graham suddenly realized Sam was holding him back with force. They struggled.

"Graham—stop!"

"I need to know. *Tala* needs to know!"

The door swung open suddenly, and there Dalton stood. Both he and Clarisse were in sanitary suits. That's when the seriousness of the situation hit Graham, and he and Sam both stumbled backward, gaining as much distance as they could from the child in the clear box at the far corner of the room. Clarisse leaned over the box; a bright light shone from within it. The room was warm.

"Graham, I'm sorry it has to be like this," said Dalton. "It's a girl, and so far she's healthy. Now please, for your daughter's sake, let Clarisse do what she needs to do."

Graham nodded, standing as Dalton closed the door and longing to hold the new life—*his daughter*—on the other side. Sam reached out to give Graham a consoling pat as McCann appeared in the hallway.

"Clarisse! *Clarisse!* It's Tala—she's hemorrhaging!"

Graham ran into the room to find Tala pale as death. "No!" he yelled.

Macy, stricken with fear, sopped up the bright red blood flowing from beneath Tala's body.

"Graham?" Tala said reaching for him.

He held her, putting his mouth close to her ear. She was cold and weak. Someone pounded on a door down the hall. He heard more yelling.

"Graham?" she said again.

He looked her in the eyes and tried to smile. "Tala." He swallowed. "It's a girl. She's beautiful, like you. She's healthy. They're keeping her safe. Please . . . please hold on. You'll see her soon."

"Why didn't you tell me?" Clarisse yelled at McCann as she entered the room.

"It just started!" he yelled back.

Graham held Tala. He could tell she was fading. Death was a familiar fiend by now. He recognized its hallmark in an instant.

The syringes and medicinal scents moved beyond Graham's periphery. He cradled Tala's head in his arms, paying no attention to what they were doing. She hung onto his arms, but her hold was weakening. If these were to be her final moments, he would selfishly steal them as his own to keep inside until his own last days.

"Where's the afterbirth?" Clarisse yelled order after order. "There's got to be a missing piece. Administer the oxytocin! Start the IV! Macy, begin packing her. She's type O; who's got it? Let's get a line going!"

They tugged at Tala's body, but Graham held her attention. The room began to fill with all the strangers who'd become family. He held her still. She was pale, and her blue lips trembled with cold, but she continued to stare into him. She knew.

"She's a girl?" Tala managed a weak smile.

"Yes," he whispered, stroking her ebony hair away from her pale face.

Tala clutched at his shirt with her left arm and pulled his lips toward hers, kissing him gently. "I love you, Graham. You're going to be a wonderful father." She enunciated each syllable with fading breath. Her eyes began to blink.

"Tala? *Tala!*" He asked it at first, then screamed her name in anguish as her eyes closed for eternity. "Clarisse! *Do something!*" When he stood up, the sight of all the blood covering Clarisse and the others trying to help her nearly made him faint.

Clarisse paid no attention. She frantically began heart compressions. Macy began crying while McCann continued to push blood, coming directly from Sam, into Tala's veins. But she was lost.

34

Devastation

"It's been nearly a week," Harding said. "I realize your people are devastated after the death of Tala, but we need to get answers from your prisoners or let them go."

Dalton stared at the dust clumps gathered beneath Harding's metal desk. Yes, *devastated*. Everyone now walked in a zombie-like state from morning till night.

If it hadn't been for the infant to care for, Clarisse might fade away, too. It had all happened so fast, and she blamed herself. Tala had never even gotten to see her own child. And Graham? He wasn't even human at the moment. He didn't sleep, but sat outside of the child's door day and night when he wasn't standing at Tala's freshly mounded grave. If the baby didn't exist, neither would Graham, and Dalton couldn't blame him one bit.

So far the baby girl, as yet unnamed, had not so much as ran a temperature.

"We're not letting them go," Dalton said and lifted his eyes just enough to send Harding an ominous look. He let it sink in before saying anything else. "They know where we are, now, even though they were unconscious when we brought them here. It's too much of a risk. Besides, they'd slit our throats the moment we turned our back on them. I'm not letting them go only to have to deal with them another day. No, we'll do the responsible thing and execute them when we're done."

Dalton gave Harding time to rebut, but Harding only tapped his pencil on the desk. Dalton resisted the urge to seize his damn pencil and snap it in half.

"How is Clarisse holding up?"

Dalton took a deep breath. He shook his head. "She's having a very tough time. We all are." Standing to leave, he said, "Henry, I'll let you know as soon as we have any information from the terrorists. We're not letting them go. Let us deal with things our own way."

"Wait. How's the infant?"

Dalton stopped and turned to answer him. "So far, she's healthy. We're watching for the virus around the clock. Clarisse is giving it two weeks to show up. We'll keep you posted."

"Was she born with the antibodies?"

"Yes, some. She's also been inoculated. She could still come down with it at this point, though."

"Must be tough for Graham," Harding said crossing his arms across his chest.

"It's a whole new kind of hell," Dalton whispered in a choked voice as he left the room.

35

Mourning

"I'll take care of the baby, Clarisse. You go ahead to the lab. Macy and I can handle her," McCann said as he recognized Clarisse's dilemma. She hadn't slept more than a few hours total in the many days since Tala's death. Everyone was falling apart. Graham sat outside the baby's room in a chair, often with a weeping Bang in his lap. He didn't talk.

Marcy and Mark had taken over Bang's care. To say the boy was distraught was an understatement. He said almost nothing, made muffled cries, delirious in pain. He and Graham both resembled zombies. Looking at Graham in despair, Macy asked, "What are we going to do?"

"I don't know," Mark responded.

He didn't have an answer. His own heart felt as if it had been impaled on something; a sharp pain in his chest constantly reminded him of the wonderful mother Tala had been, even to him, and how they'd lost her. The baby would never know the pleasure of having Tala to care for her.

It was the greatest wrong Graham had ever experienced. It just shouldn't be this way. He blindly patted Bang on the back in a vague effort toward comfort, though he himself was lost. His grief had stolen his soul; only his physical form remained. Since the birth he had hardly left the baby's doorway.

In short, McCann found himself as leader of Graham's wounded gang. He kept them all fed and rested. He had led Graham home from Tala's grave, mindless in pain. He rocked Bang to sleep, and looked in on the motherless infant in the incubator. Wearing fitted gloves, he changed her diaper and fed her from a bottle sometimes, though Macy had taken over most of the baby's daytime tasks. It had been almost a week, and no one was yet ready to move forward in even the simplest of ways. They all held fast to the anguish within themselves.

They lived in a hell that McCann doubted they could climb out of, and his own strength was fading after caring for everyone night and day. It trickled away a little at a time like a leak from a reservoir.

Clarisse gazed at the sleeping infant through the plastic. The baby was perfect in every way. So far, they'd gotten away with calling her "the baby," but soon Graham was going to have to give the child a name.

McCann stood silently at Clarisse side, watching the baby's chest rise and fall as she lay on her back, both hands balled into tiny fists as if she tried to hold on to something unseen.

"Yes," Clarisse said, wiping the back of her gloved hand across her eyes. "I'll go to the lab for a few hours and return around lunchtime. I'll check on her then, but use the radio if you need anything. She has another week in there, but so far she's perfect. Keep checking her temperature on the hour and write it down in the log. Don't try to remember it, you'll forget. We're all sleep deprived." She handed him the clipboard where they noted all of the baby's details from around-the-clock observation.

As if he'd forget to write anything down. "I've got it covered Clarisse. Go ahead. Go."

She nodded and opened the door, revealing Graham's silent form sitting in the wooden chair, Bang asleep in his lap. Graham's eyes locked on the child in the box as Clarisse closed the door behind her and addressed him. "Graham, you know, you can go in and see her any time. Just suit up. There's an extra suit beside the door. She has one week to go, but after that you'll need to hold her—*a lot*. Take care of her, you know?"

McCann heard the encouraging words through the cracked door as he mixed up another bottle of formula for the baby's next feeding. Graham would come around. He just needed time to recover from the shock of losing Tala. They all needed that time. McCann hoped they had enough of it before the terrorists found them.

36

Loss

I s this my fault? I should have taken her blood pressure that morning instead of running off to the lab. I might have caught an increase, I might have detected preeclampsia.

Walking the worn path between their residence and the lab, Clarisse allowed her questions to flow and feelings of guilt to spill forth.

My God, it was preventable. I let her die. I could have stopped her death had I not been so involved in coming up with the virus. I allowed her to die. It was my fault . . .

Morbid thoughts ran through her mind. Seeing Tala's blood rushing out of her, her olive skin turning pale and then turning blue. Hearing the baby's insistent cries from the next room, Graham's stricken expression, and yelling *No!* over and over. She could hear the despairing echo still.

She wiped her eyes and took a deep breath before she entered the lab. When she looked up, she found Dalton leaning against the far wall of the room, a worried expression on his face. They'd met like this every morning. He tried to extinguish her guilt, her pain. He felt it too. They all did. They'd lost Tala, but they'd gained a life, and they desperately needed to survive.

"You're early," he said.

"McCann and Macy have the baby covered."

Dalton thrust forward and took steps toward Clarisse; they fell into an embrace. She leaned back after a moment and looked up at him. "You can't . . . fix me, Dalton. I can barely breathe with this pain of her death. I feel so guilty." She started to cry again. Her eyes had never been so swollen.

Trying to contain his own emotion, he said, "You're not at fault, Clarisse. No one blames you one bit for what happened. How can you think that way?"

She brushed him off and put on her lab coat. "I've got work to do now. Have you guys gotten anything out of the prisoners?"

"No. Not much anyway. Rick and Reuben both know a little Arabic and we caught the prisoners talking last night on film. They're trying to translate it."

"They can't see each other in separate stalls. How did that happen?"

"We conveniently left the doors cracked a little—by accident on purpose. They talked."

"Gotcha," she said, but worried they were taking chances.

"How's your progress?" Dalton asked.

She let a deep breath out. "I'm getting closer. It shouldn't be too long now. I might have something to work with, in another two weeks."

She now ignored her conscience, the potential consequences of her actions when it came to this. It was the only way to cope with the underlying morality of their plan.

"Clarisse?"

She looked up from her desk.

"I love you. We'll get through this. It won't be long now."

She looked away and nodded, ignoring any further communication with Dalton. She was coping with too much right now; any more and she might break. And she couldn't afford to break. Not now. Not yet.

As Dalton left she turned back to her work. She wouldn't leave the lab until the nightfall.

37

Tehya

The dirt had already settled a bit on Tala's mound after only a few days. Graham left at sunrise, gathering wildflowers that bloomed in front of their borrowed home. He couldn't bear to lie in bed anymore. He smelled her there; he smelled her everywhere. He heard her laugh. She whispered to him on the wind.

As he'd passed the opened door of the baby's room, Graham caught a glimpse of Macy cooing at the infant. He imagined the baby sucking on a bottle. His eyes lingered on the worn doorknob in the low morning light. He turned and padded down the hall with his chest tight, his heart tighter.

Today was the day he could finally hold her, and yet he wasn't certain he wanted to. This brought a profound feeling of guilt because Tala, more than anyone, would want him to love the child beyond measure. The truth was, Graham loved Tala beyond measure and having lost her too, like his first love, he felt like he didn't have it in him to love like that again.

No, instead he would care for the child. He would raise her, but he would never love again. Not her, not anyone. That's how it was right now. And when the child grew up, he would leave and find his place in death and be happy about it. In the meantime, he would only go on for Tala.

Her name was Tehya, meaning "precious." This was the girl name they'd settled on weeks ago. Even though he'd given Tala a hard time about the odd name, he now agreed she was a precious child.

Bending down, Graham lay the blossoms atop the mound while brushing the perished ones aside. The constriction in his chest thrust forward and ruptured into wretched mourning. No longer would he feel the slickness of Tala's braided, glistening black hair warmed in the sunlight. No longer would he hear the old Indian tales she often repeated for the children in dull moments of their workday. Her smile would exist only in his memory now. She loved the cabin in Cascade, and she would never see it again. Nor would she see the child she gave her life to have.

The love Graham had invested had been ripped from him so quickly. The pain was so deep; he would never be whole again. He resented the child right now. He wished she'd not lived so that he could die too.

A wind blew off the lake, chilling him. Graham dried his eyes with the back of his hand, taking long, deep breaths to calm his raging heart. But he'd promised her. The child lived, and he would carry on.

38

The Prisoners

Dalton and Sam watched the footage and listened to the audio feed again and again. The speech came over as feminine. There was no mistaking it, the leader of this group was the woman. They were all a little surprised when Rick played them the footage the first time. When they met her behind the bars in the light of day, she pretended to be meek and subservient, as if she'd been a captive. It was all an act. She was hell-bent on murder, and made sure the other two men were complying with the kill-the-infidels agenda.

"I'll be damned," Sam said. "Though I guess it's not surprising, since she was fully armed when we kidnapped her. They wouldn't have let her see the light of day if she didn't have some skill set they found redeeming."

"See what I mean?" Rick asked. "She might look like a sweet, innocent girl, but that woman is evil. Don't be fooled fellas."

"What is she saying, exactly?" Sam asked.

"Same thing as always—*Allahu Akbar*, praise be to God. Only it's meant as a war cry," Rick said.

"You'd think they'd get a little more creative than that after all this time," Sam said.

Rick leaned forward, "Yeah, well you have to give it to them—they're consistent. Why mess with success?"

"That's only because there's no depth, no limitation to the atrocities they are willing to commit." Sam's voice dropped to a whisper. "Slicing a five-year-old in half was only the beginning. Committing genocide on a global scale . . ." He couldn't finish the sentence because he lacked the eloquence with which to express his astonished disgust.

They took their turns in this comprehension of the events that had led them here. Each time those actions were mulled over, annotated, the indigestible realization came around; then it sped off into the universe to return once more. True answers never really came.

Rick addressed the silence, "Don't try to understand them, Sam. It'll drive you insane. The problem is, you're applying human standards, and they're not human; they can't be. They gave that option up long ago. As for these clowns, we have to keep up the questioning to buy Clarisse more time. She's nearly done, and the testing will start soon. Even so, I doubt the interrogation will give us anything we can use."

"Good. I'm ready to leave this place. It's starting to give me the creeps."

"What do you mean?" Rick asked, not knowing Sam to be creeped out easily.

He shook his head. "Tala's death. She's still . . . *here* to me. She used to stroke the top of my daughter's head and kiss her there. Last night, Addy woke up and swore she felt Tala do that as she slept. She was convinced of it. It took me forever to get her calmed down. I don't believe in ghosts, but I do believe in strong spirits and Tala had—or *has*—a very strong spirit."

Rick was silent, staring at the door leading to the prisoner's cells. "She certainly left us too soon. I don't know if Graham can go on after this. I can't imagine losing Olivia. She's all torn up about not having known what to do. She was right there with Tala."

"Graham *will* go on. I've been there. As soon as he holds the little one, he'll go on—for Tala."

Rick blew out a breath. "Does he have a choice?" It was a rhetorical question, but Sam shook his head anyway.

Just then Dalton entered the building; they recognized the sound of his footsteps, unlike anyone else's. They all knew each other that way by now, each man coming and going, their identities revealed in their footfalls.

"Hey. How are the infidels today?" Dalton joked.

Rick answered, "We're fine. The asshats, on the other hand, were up late last night. Regurgitating the same old rant. Sounded more like a pep talk, though. And guess what? The ringleader is the lady."

"You're sure?" Dalton asked.

"Yep."

Rick turned to Dalton. "How's Graham this morning?"

Dalton shook his head. It was too soon to ask.

Just then a cart carrying the prisoners' daily breakfast came through the front door. Rick and Sam greeted the guard and accepted the food, then pushed the cart smelling of pancakes down the hall to the cells.

Dalton wandered down the hallway and watched as Rick slid the trays of food under the bars. The prisoners didn't move. Instead they sat with their backs against the cinderblock wall of their cells. The female prisoner appeared wary; the two men both had half smiles on their faces. No one spoke, but only followed Rick with their eyes as he delivered the food.

Dalton peeked in on each one. They were all being treated humanely: enough water, food, and the use of a bathroom facility. A small slice of sunshine came through a tiny window at the top of each cell. Once a day, Rick led them to a small enclosed courtyard with chained arms and legs. They didn't struggle, but remained confident. They were waiting. All they had to do was wait for the disease to spread north to save them.

Dalton walked away in disgust. If he stayed any longer, he'd do something he'd regret.

He couldn't wait for Clarisse, as brilliant as she was, to finish her research and help them exterminate the terrorists once and for all. They were almost at that point.

In Dalton's mind, the terrorists were responsible for Tala's death and the circumstances leading up to it. They were certainly responsible for Steven's. Hell, as he saw it, they were responsible for everything.

39

A Sign of Him

Lucy and Marcy came by the nursery to relieve Macy and McCann for a few hours so they could resume the search for the dogs. As Macy said good-bye, she gave directions to Marcy about the baby's last feeding of the day.

"Please don't go," Bang pleaded. "Can I come with you?"

"We're just going to search for Sheriff again. You know we do that every day. We're going to looking on the west side today, hoping for some tracks. Doesn't Addy want you to stay with her?"

"No, she's helping Olivia. Please, can I come?"

Macy looked up to McCann, who nodded. "Go let Ms. Olivia know you're coming with us—and make sure you put your boots on."

Bang ran off, and she watched as he flung his legs far ahead of him, his desire to go with them so strong.

"He needs some time away. It'll be good for him," McCann said as he readied the horses.

Macy agreed and, knowing they needed some good news, she hoped they'd find something, some sign of Sheriff or even the other dogs. She tucked some supplies into a backpack and McCann cupped his hands together as a foot lift. They performed this routine nearly every day, and could easily predict one another's actions. Macy likened it to being married; she couldn't imagine another living soul this close to her, the way a man and woman in love lived their lives side by side every day. Then, as it often did, came the reminder that Graham had lost Tala. It used to be that she couldn't hold back this pain, but now she could stop it at the base of her throat, right before the tears began.

Bang returned, and McCann scooped him up and settled him in front of Macy on her horse.

After McCann mounted, they veered west outside the main gate. They'd covered the east thoroughly in recent weeks and had found nothing. The guards waved them through as they passed the gate. Instead of acting suspicious about their endeavors, as in the past, nowadays the guards wished them luck on departure and asked them what they'd seen out there upon return. They seemed curious about what lay beyond the gates. Why they never ventured out and bucked the rules was something she could not fathom. Where was their determination? They had the desire, she could see it in their eyes, the way they gazed out at the same scenery day after day.

She'd finally came to the conclusion that it was just as Sam had said when she'd questioned him about their behavior: the residents of Hope were cut from a different cloth.

They crossed the road, and Macy followed McCann's down an embankment and up the other side. Her horse easily traversed the ditch, and she held Bang tightly with one arm; the boy, following Macy's example, leaned backward as the horse leaned forward.

Once under the dense forest canopy, they spoke in soft whispers while keeping their eyes open for signs. The shaded air chilled Macy's bare shoulders. From time to time, she would watch McCann's profile as he turned right and then left, scanning the forest floor. His jaw flexed as he gnawed on one of the toothpicks he'd whittled from a clean stick during the quiet evening hours.

McCann would stop occasionally, study one spot, and then continue on, sometimes explaining what he saw and sometimes not. This was their customary routine on these searches. But at one stop he lingered, then descended from his horse after a few moments.

"What is it?" Macy asked. McCann walked over to the edge of the deer trail they'd followed and investigated something out of Macy's view along the forest floor. She was afraid to hope anymore, so she didn't; she refused to let her conscience be had.

"Could be nothing," he said, emerging from the undergrowth. Macy thought he was getting ready to remount his horse, but instead, he removed the stick from his mouth and placed it in his shirt pocket. Then, without warning, he placed two fingers into his mouth and whistled long and high. It was a whistle he'd used many times to call Sheriff home back in Cascade. It startled Macy and Bang, and even her horse took a step backward.

"Did you see something?"

Instead of answering, McCann repeated the whistle, this time even louder.

"McCann?"

Once more he let out a whistle, then turned to her after a few seconds of silence. "They were here. I can see their tracks. They're older tracks, but they were *here*, Macy." McCann pointed to the ground and the brush nearby.

He walked a few paces and pulled back some of the greenery covering the ground to study the tracks. "There was someone else here too. Boot prints." He handed Macy his horse's reins and followed the tracks on foot.

Hope swallowed Macy so hard that she could barely breathe.

McCann knelt down and ran his hand over the ground. "They're probably a few weeks old, probably from that bad rain we had. They could be anywhere by now." He looked at Macy. "Don't look so crestfallen. This is good news. At least we found a sign of them."

Bang leaned back into Macy. She knew he was feeling a loss of hope too. They were *so close*.

McCann whistled again. They waited for a response, but none ever came. Reluctantly they returned back to Hope

But McCann's words echoed in Macy's ears: *At least we found a sign of them.*

40

Holding Her

Later that afternoon, Graham passed by the doorway of
Tehya's room. "Graham, come in," said Clarisse. She'd come
home early that afternoon to bring the baby out of quarantine for the first time.

Mark swung the bedroom door open a little wider for Graham to
step inside.

"I'm going to open the incubator. Do you want to hold your
daughter?" Clarisse said.

He wasn't sure what he wanted other than Tala alive and here
with him. "I . . ." His voice came out raspy and pained. He shook his
head.

"Graham! She's your daughter!" Marcy scolded him, angry tears
running down her cheeks. "Tala would want you to hold her now.
She'd *hate* you for this!"

Tears came to Graham at the mention of her name. He'd been

numb for days and hadn't realized how much everyone else was grieving, nor had he cared, but hearing Marcy so upset with him shook him a little, and he opened his arms for her to come near. He hugged the young lady. Yes, she had given him some teenage trouble in the past, but what she'd said just now was right. He couldn't neglect the baby; Tala would, in fact, be furious with him. He owed it to her, and he owed it to Tehya. The infant hadn't asked to be brought into this screwed up mess of a world, but yet she was here now, and she was his responsibility no matter how much pain he was in over the loss of her mother. "I'm sorry. I'm sorry, Marcy," he said.

"It's okay," she said sniffing. "Just . . . *come back to us*. We need you."

The baby chose that moment to cry out in hunger. Her little fists rose to her mouth as she tried to find something to suck on.

"She's hungry. Would you like to feed her?" Clarisse asked.

Marcy stepped away and wiped her tears. Graham took a deep breath and Clarisse stood over the opened incubator, holding a bottle full of formula. Wrapped in a blanket she battled to kick off, Tehya's cries became more urgent; from the moment she was born they had tugged at his heart.

"Go ahead, pick her up," Marcy urged.

"Let him take his time, Marcy," Mark said.

Graham brushed his index finger along her baby soft cheek, and Tehya turned in his direction.

"She's hungry," Clarisse repeated, now farther away.

He could only see Tehya as his daughter now, her dark, shiny hair so like her mother's, her little nose and mouth. "Shhh," he said and reached down with his large, clumsy hands to pick up her tiny body. He slipped one hand under her small round head and the other under her bottom and cradled her up toward his chest. Her warm body squirmed in his hold. Her little heart vibrated strongly against him. He sat with her in the chair by the window and Clarisse handed him the bottle. He brushed it against her lips and soon the baby greedily suckled. He hadn't heard anyone leave the room, but by the time she was finished with the bottle, he found himself alone with his daughter in his arms; her bright coal eyes stared up at him in wonder as he began to hum one of the many songs Tala sang during her days. And somewhere within his heart it hurt just a little less than it had before.

41

Progress

"Ask him where they first landed in the States," Rick said to Reuben.

"I don't know all of those words, man," Reuben said and ran a hand over his face in frustration. "Look, the kid's tired. We've kept him up for two days straight now. This is cruel."

Rick couldn't believe what he was hearing from Reuben. "This is cruel? So, we're keeping him from sleeping? After everything they've done to us, you think this is cruel?"

"I'm just saying it's below us, that's all," Reuben said.

"Sometimes I don't get you, man. It's only sleep deprivation," Rick muttered while watching the kid, who leaned against his cell wall blinking his eyes; each time his lids slid down over the corneas for a longer stretch of time. "Hey!" Rick yelled and startled both the kid and Reuben.

Reuben got up and left the room.

"Fine," Rick said. *That guy is losing it.*

"Kid, you tired? Sleepy?" Rick asked, nodding his head. The young man must have gotten the gist of what Rick was asking and nodded back.

"Too bad."

"Allahu Akbar," the young terrorist said in a sleepy tone.

"Yeah, yeah . . . How about you tell me where you arrived when you came to this cursed land you hate so much?"

The boy's eyelids began to bob again and soon his dark curly head followed the movement.

"Crap," Rick muttered and rose from his chair to get a glass of water. As he passed the cell of the man next door, he heard him say, "He . . . don't . . . know."

Rick stopped in his tracks. The light was dim in the cell. "You speak English."

"Some" came the reply.

"What's your name?"

The man snorted and laughed a bit. "Names? Names no longer matter, but they called me Omar."

"True. Why don't you tell me the answers to the questions I tried to get out of him, Omar?"

"We arrived all over. In every airport of this country. Even by sea. Each team has its job: to exterminate or imprison the leftovers until our task is done."

"You speak better English than you let on. You're not Arabic."

"I am not."

"Why did you join them?" Rick thought he saw something like shame, though he couldn't be sure. This man had a conscious, a rarity among these animals. Though the light was dim in his cell, the whites of his eyes looked down as if the answers were there on the concrete floor.

"There isn't a good reason anymore. Everything I was running from is now gone. They killed them all. I, myself, killed many." He paused, then pointed to the sleeping kid in the next cell. "This kid is brainwashed. He will tell you nothing. This woman next to me will slit your throat if you turn your back on her. She's killed children, pregnant mothers, in the most horrific ways. She's honored among them, but even they know she is insane; a revered oddity. I know you will kill us. I ask you to just do it now. But know your days are numbered here. They will kill all of you, and then they will kill themselves. Evil has a way of triumphing even among those who use its will."

Rick thought he might be dreaming this. He shook his head. The more the man talked, the more his accent started sounding almost Italian. His appearance wasn't anything he'd question. He certainly looked Arabic. He knew there were many Americans who turned traitorous and joined the Islamist terrorists, as well as many Europeans seeking adventures among killers. It never made any sense to him.

"Why are you saying this now?"

As the man began to speak, his voice tightened with emotion. "I don't want to return to them. If there is anything good left, let it be a warning to you to leave here. Go north. Live the remaining days hiding from them, if you can, or end it all now. Leave nothing for them to take."

Rick shook his head as he left the lockup. It was too much. He began to wonder if perhaps he was sleep-deprived and was imagining all of this.

42

A Weapon Is Born

"So what does this do, exactly?" Dalton asked Clarisse. He checked to make sure the lab door was locked so that no one might accidently come in and disturb their very private conference. Sam, Reuben, Graham, and Rick were also in attendance, each having snuck into the lab at various times over the last half hour.

"Is it a completely new virus?" Reuben asked.

Clarisse pushed her glasses up the bridge of her nose. Dalton loved it when she did that.

"It's a mutation of the existing virus. I've manipulated it to attach to the antibody markers from the hosts we collected." Dalton looked around the room at the blank stares.

"Let's say the terrorists have carrier captives. They've never contracted the virus, and they were never given the terrorists' vaccine. They should be okay. This virus will pass them over, since they don't have the same markers in their antibodies. It's a selective virus. A *deadly* selective virus."

Dalton watched for Reuben's reaction more than anyone else. He knew Reuben wouldn't be comfortable with the plan, but what were they to do—die off because the terrorists said so? To hell with that.

Reuben shifted in his seat, asking, "So, how many will this thing kill?"

Dalton thought that Reuben was probably trying to reconcile this genocide in his own mind. Before Clarisse could answer, he interrupted. He wanted that answer to come from him so that she wouldn't be the one to blame. "*All* of them. *Every last one of them.* Whoever has received their vaccine will perish of this manipulated virus as it spreads over the globe."

The room remained silent for a time.

"Damn . . . that's dangerous." It was Sam who finally said something, in a solemn whisper.

"Don't you think *they* had one of these meetings?" Reuben asked, clearly agitated. What makes us any better than them if we go through with this? What keeps this from mutating and coming back to bite us in the ass?"

"Come on, Reuben. That's not exactly fair," Rick interjected.

"Sure it's fair. Are we not also terrorists if we commit this crime?"

Dalton struck back, "What would you have us do? Do you have any better ideas? Look, I know you're uncomfortable with this. Hell, I'm uncomfortable with it too, but we have no choice. They've already killed most of us. Think about that. I shouldn't have to remind you of it. They've already murdered over ninety-eight percent of the human race! We don't have a choice anymore! Nothing else will work!"

More silence ensued after Dalton stopped shouting.

"Reuben, I too have a difficult time with this," added Graham, "but let me just say I'm willing to accept this evil deed so that our children and others can live their lives. I'll bear the burden of this crime until I die, but I'll do so, so that they can live again."

Reuben let out a long, slow breath. "And what if *I* can't live with it?"

Dalton shook his head. "That's a decision that you will have to make for yourself. This *is* the plan. We're ready to implement it now. So if you're not with us, please leave and don't stand in our way."

Reuben shook his head. "I need to think about this," he said, leaving the room with a slam of the door.

Everyone stole glances at the other faces around them. Dalton's face glowed red hot with anger. It was a tough decision, but any thought of his own kids told him it was the right one.

43

Deserter

Rick had waited hours in the lockup for Reuben to relieve him of guard duty. He bounced a little rubber ball against the painted cinderblock wall. In his mind, he knew what must have happened, yet he didn't want to believe it was true. Finally, Sam walked in, the next up as guard. When he saw Rick, he asked the obvious question: "Where's Reuben?"

Without breaking his rhythm with the ball, Rick said, "I'm pretty sure I know, but someone should check his quarters. Did you see Lavinda or his daughters this morning at breakfast?"

"Um, no, but that's not unusual. Sometimes they make their own breakfast at home."

"Yeah, but something tells me this is different. Do you want to go check and see if they're at home, or should I?"

"You think they left after the meeting yesterday?"

Rick shook his head and caught the ball in his fist one last time. "I'm pretty sure that might be it. Reuben's always been—how should I say it—a little more moral than the rest of us. To a fault, he's a moral man. That's not a bad thing, but in a time like *this,* it's a bad thing.

"You don't think he would rat on us, do you?"

Rick thought for a moment, "I hadn't considered that. That would jeopardize everything." He rose from his chair to let Sam take over. "I'll check it out. The prisoners were still asleep, last time I checked. Nothing new." He left the room and headed for Reuben's home.

Once he reached the line of homes, he scanned the area. This time of day, Reuben's wife Lavinda often helped out in the main house, taking care of the children.

He saw Olivia standing in the kitchen kneading bread dough as a few of the children watched. "Hi Livy, have you seen Lavinda or Reuben's girls today?" He'd tried to sound calm, but he was out of breath.

Olivia looked up at Rick, then did a double take when she recognized his urgent expression. "I can't say that I have, now that you're asking. Why?"

He looked around. "You haven't seen them at all?"

She shook her head. "Maybe they're taking a long morning to themselves."

"Yeah, maybe that's it," he conceded.

Rick headed to Reuben's family's house, knocking twice on the door. "Shit," he said under his breath, knowing full well what was going on. He tried the door and found it had been left unlocked—something Reuben would never do. "Reuben!" he yelled into the darkened living room. "Lavinda? Lawoaka?" Nothing. No one was home. He walked in farther and saw that their belongings were gone; the kitchen was devoid of food and supplies. They'd left. On the kitchen table he found a note addressed to Dalton.

"God dammit!"

Knowing Dalton was probably in Clarisse's office at this time, he headed there first.

The townspeople looked up from their daily routine as Rick passed them; some of them waved. He tried not to look so intense, knowing that any unwanted attention might bring further suspicion.

Then one of the guards stopped him. "Rick, is there something wrong?"

"Ah no, I'm just trying to get a little exercise as I run errands this morning. It's been a while." *Yeah, that didn't sound suspicious at all.*

"Okay. Don't hurt yourself!"

Smartass, he thought. "Nah, see ya later!"

After that, he took it a little easier realizing that he was, in fact, drawing unwanted attention. He rounded the corner to Clarisse's lab and took a deep breath before entering.

Clarisse was bent over a microscope, as usual, and Dalton worked at a desk with his head down. "Uh . . . hi!" Rick said.

"Hey, what's up?" Dalton said.

Rick made sure to close the door securely behind him and then took out Reuben's note and walked toward Dalton. "Reuben left this for you. It looks like they cleared out last night."

"What?" Dalton said as he reached for the note.

"Yeah man, they're gone. All their stuff's gone including the food in the kitchen and the truck in front of their house. They packed up and left."

"Reuben *left*?" Clarisse asked.

"Yeah, I don't think he could handle our plan," Rick said while Dalton read the note to himself.

"Sonofabitch! Where are the prisoners?" Dalton said.

"Did he tell Harding?" Clarisse asked.

Dalton held up a hand to stem the questions while he scanned the note. "It looks like he left Harding a note too. Quick, we've got to act now. It might already be too late. Clarisse, go ahead and give the prisoners the virus, we might not get another chance. Rick, come with me. Let's try to run interference to give her enough time before it's too late."

44

A Deception

Harding took his time on his morning run. Not only did he go the extra mile today, but he found he'd been pushing himself more in general lately. It was probably out of frustration. That or his lack of control when it came to the things he wanted. What he wanted was Clarisse, though that wasn't going to happen and he could see that clearly now. This realization still made him frustrated, so he ran at a steady pace and continued well past his normal route.

He told himself he'd have to refocus. The town of Hope needed him. There was nothing more he could do other than be a symbol of the future yet to come. Now that his citizens were safe from the virus they could venture out more. He hoped that finally they would believe there was a future for them and possibly begin to procreate again.

Unless, of course, what the Americans had said about the terrorists was true. He let his mind settle after a while, paying attention only to the cadence of his shoes slapping against the pavement. All else he tuned out; the thought of terrorists responsible for global genocide was too much to consider.

Harding found himself changing direction back toward his house after he could no longer keep up a steady pace and showered off before heading into work. There was much to be done in the days ahead. They needed to ramp up their food preservation activities for the harvest that would soon be coming in, and since they were now immune to the virus, thanks to the Americans, they could begin taking overnight trips to various areas to secure more supplies and see what was going on out in the rest of the world. Perhaps they could pick up more survivors. The first trip would most likely be to Vancouver, and he needed to get a group ready for that. How to conceal their missions from the terrorists he hadn't quite figured out yet. He certainly didn't want to lead them directly to Hope.

Once showered and dressed, Harding headed to his office. He would check in on Clarisse later in the afternoon. Even though he knew she was attached to Dalton, he still cared about her, and her mourning over Tala's death weighed on him.

As he walked, he saw Rick jogging toward Clarisse's office when one of the guards stopped to talk to him. Rick was an odd one but seemed nice enough. Harding didn't interrupt their conversation and continued on as Rick waved good-bye to the guard and continued on his journey.

Once he sat down behind his desk, Harding noticed a folded note with his name scribbled in pen across the top. He didn't recognize the handwriting and so, intrigued, he sat down and opened up the letter.

A moment later, the paper slid between his fingers and fell to the floor beside his desk. He thought of Clarisse and only Clarisse. *Could Dalton have possibly made her do this?* He looked out his window facing the lake and saw the trees, now bearing fruit. He took a deep breath and picked up the phone. He knew this would be the last peaceful second before a chaotic storm.

"Lock down the base. Imminent threat."

Sirens immediately sounded, piercing the tranquil quiet of what had started as just another ordinary day.

45

Last Chance

Clarisse quickly grabbed the syringes prefilled with the virus from the refrigerator. As Rick ran out the door with his weapon drawn, the sirens began to blare. Dalton stopped in his tracks and looked back at Clarisse. "Go!" he shouted, and she bolted out the back door.

Clarisse sprinted toward the lockup building. Soldiers were scattering, and residents looked confused and afraid. Once she got to the prison doors the guards stood in front of her, blocking entry. "Henry sent me here to stay inside, said there was a threat in the main building."

"We're not supposed to let anyone through."

She tried again. "Look, that's what Harding told me to do, he was worried I might get attacked."

The soldiers looked at one another and then one of them motioned her through. "Just stay inside, in case something happens."

She looked back at him, and one soldier shook his head and

mumbled something to the other. She'd played on their sense of confusion, and so far it had worked.

Once inside she locked the main door behind her and saw Sam watching out the window.

"What the hell is going on?"

"I have to give the prisoners the *special vaccine* now, right now. Block the door."

"You shouldn't go back there alone."

"We don't have much choice. They're going to stop us at any minute. Buy as much time as you can."

She ran for the lockup cells in the back and saw that the prisoners were awake and confused by the loud alarms.

"Good morning," she said out of breath and tried a bright smile though her hands were shaking. "Everything's fine, it's just a drill," she said though she doubted they understood her words, she hoped her body language conveyed nonchalant ease.

"I've got a flu shot for you guys. It's mandatory for everyone on base. If you'll just come to the side here, I'll give it to you and then Sam will bring you your breakfast."

The young boy walked over sleepily. He shook his head no to Clarisse in protest of the shot.

She shook her head. "No shot, no food."

The kid looked to the others, and the older man nodded his head for the young man to comply.

Clarisse had hesitated a second before she plunged the needle into his arm muscle. Though her stomach clenched for what she just condemned this life to, she continued. Next, the woman merely sat staring daggers at Clarisse. The man said something in Arabic, encouraging her to comply. The woman reluctantly got up and sauntered toward the bars. She moved her arm toward Clarisse, who immediately injected the virus into her arm, but just as she removed the needle, the woman reached through with her other arm and grabbed Clarisse around the neck, pulling her to the grate. Reaching through with her other arm, she wrapped her forearm around Clarisse's throat to choke her. She braced her feet up on the bars in order to exert the most force in her effort to strangle Clarisse.

Clarisse struggled and tried to fight her off but, admittedly, her assailant had an excellent hold on her. Clarisse's vision started to fade, and she knew it was only a matter of time before she'd black out completely.

Suddenly a man's hand pulled on the woman jihadist. Clarisse thought Sam must have heard the commotion and come from the front room. Freed, Clarisse fell to her knees on the concrete ground, heaved large breaths. She looked around, but Sam wasn't there.

Instead, the woman was screaming something incomprehensible and kicking at the bars. The other prisoner that she'd yet to give the virus to held the female terrorist by her arms as she flung her limbs toward Clarisse in another attempt to grab her.

The man smiled at her, though he continued to hold the attacker until Clarisse was clear of her reach through the bars.

"Thank you," she tried to say through her sore throat. "Please, please . . . don't kill her." The other woman continued to spit and hurl vile deciphered threats against her. He shook his head in amusement and then flung the woman to the floor of her cell.

There was a great commotion outside, and Sam yelled, "Clarisse, hurry up! They're coming!"

The man behind the bars waved to her to approach. He seemed to somehow know. She retrieved the last syringe from where it landed on the floor, looking confused at the man. He smiled at her.

"You know?" she said.

"You must hurry," was all he said as he lifted his sleeve.

She pushed in the needle that would take his life and the lives of many others in time. She pressed the plunger on the syringe, releasing the poison into him.

Soon guards were in the lockup, yelling and pointing guns at Clarisse. She dropped everything and held her hands in the air.

"What's going on?" she yelled and feigned confusion.

One of the guards restrained her and held her hands behind her back. She let them confine her without a struggle, and then she was led out to the main room, where she saw Sam also constrained. She nodded at his questioning look, and then he diverted his gaze. One of the guards confiscated the used syringes from the floor of the prison and looked at the prisoners.

Lieutenant Harding approached, and the guard held the syringes at his eye level.

"Clarisse, What have you done?" Harding whispered to her, staring deeply into her eyes.

She didn't answer.

46

Fleeing Hope

Dalton burst through the front door. "Graham, load them up. Load everything and everyone up—*now*. We have five minutes. Leave the rest."

Graham was sitting with Tehya in his arms, feeding her, as Bang rested to the side of the living room chair. "Why? What the hell happened?"

"They found out. Reuben squealed; he couldn't just keep our plans to himself. Instead, he's jeopardized everything and put Clarisse in danger. They probably already have her locked up. I just hope she was able to give the virus to the prisoners."

"No!" Graham said. "McCann and the kids went fishing about an hour ago with the horses. They all took off this morning. I thought it was a good thing for them to do."

"Can we radio them?"

"Yeah."

Dalton thought for a minute. "That's good, actually. Quick, tell them to make it to the main road, but to hide out there until we come. Tell them *not* to come back here. Hurry, man, we have little time."

Graham nodded and took the baby with him and Bang into the back. He radioed Macy with the plan, then he packed up each and every room as fast as he could while Bang watched Tehya.

Meanwhile, Dalton had to get Clarisse and Sam back as well as free the prisoners, and he had no idea how in the world he was going to manage that. It all depended on Harding and to what extent he was willing to go. At the moment Dalton was more concerned about Clarisse and if Harding would try to use her as a bargaining chip.

Rick ran into his own home and gave Olivia the news to pack up the children and the household as fast as she could.

Soon they were throwing things into the trucks they'd brought—minus the one the Reuben had taken with him the night before. Bang remembered the chickens and hurried to round them up into boxes. Dalton packed up the food supply as Graham ran yet more stuff from Lucy and Macy's room out to the truck. In no time they were as loaded down as they had been when they came to Hope, and that was only due to their preparedness measures and the fact that they had few belongings.

Dalton was left with the items that Clarisse kept in her lab, including the vaccines and the virus she'd developed herself. He had to get to the lab, but he thought that might be where they were holding her. He would go there next after Graham and Olivia drove most of their supplies out of town and toward the kids waiting with the horses.

Dalton, loaded for bear, pounded twice on Graham's truck as Tehya cried in the backseat and Bang tried to comfort her. The guards were waiting at the closed gate. Dalton told Graham to try to reason with the guards but to bust through the gate if he had to. They doubted the guards would fire on them.

He and Rick watched the exit, and though there was shouting, the guards opened the gate and let them leave without incident. Once they were safely on the other side, Dalton and Rick made their way to the lockup.

Dalton had no idea what Harding was going to do so he simply left Rick to cover him and walked first up to lockup building, where men guarded the entrance.

"Hey, fellas. Can you let me in? I need to see how Sam is doing."

"It's on lockdown, and our orders are to detain you on sight," a guard responded.

Dalton had been pretty sure this would happen, but he was surprised when a few seconds passed and the two guards had made no move to handcuff him.

"So . . . are you going to detain me?"

The soldiers diverted their eyes from Dalton, and one said, "We haven't seen you, sir."

One of them stepped aside and Dalton quickly hurried past them and into the lockup building. As soon as he walked in, the first thing he saw was that—at the end of the long corridor past the cells—the back door stood wide open and a truck was parked in front of it. At that moment Sam rushed in the back door.

"What the hell's going on?" Dalton asked.

"They're helping us. Hurry! I've got the boy inside the truck already. The female's a bitch, though; I'm going to have to hogtie her."

That's when Dalton noticed the bloody marks on Sam's hand.

Sam glanced down at his arm. "It's nothing, the boy wanted to fight," he said dismissively.

Dalton wasn't sure what Sam might have done to the boy in the fight to get him into the truck so he asked, "Is *he* okay?"

"Yeah, he'll live—for a while anyway." He let that statement float away, with all its implications.

"It's the bitch that I'm concerned with. She tried to choke Clarisse in there, but the guy in the next cell intervened. I couldn't get back here fast enough."

Dalton was horrified. "Is Clarisse okay?"

"I don't know. I think so. It looked like she was scratched up pretty bad, but she's alive. They took her to the lab. Sorry, man. There's was nothing I could do."

Dalton nodded to the quiet man behind the bars and he wasn't surprised to see he nodded back. "Yeah, Rick said he was remorseful. I'm just thankful. He looked directly at the man. "Thank you."

The woman chanted, rocking back and forth, and the man sat solemnly atop his cot.

"Well, we can't shoot her. What are we going to do?" Dalton said.

Sam held several PlastiCuffs in his hand and said, "It's like wrestling a bear. Freight train through it, man."

"Oh great. Well, you know I've been there. She can't be that bad."

They opened the cell and it took both he and Dalton to hold her down as she tried to claw at them. She managed to bite Dalton's forearm as Sam whipped a cuff round her wrists. He was tempted to strike her across the face, but didn't.

Out of breath by the time they were through subduing her, they tossed her into the back of the truck along with the boy and then rushed back inside to get the last man. They heard shouting around the front of the building and knew their time was running out.

Once back inside, the man held his hands out for them to restrain him. Totally compliant, the prisoner even tried to rush them into fleeing when they heard more voices. Once in the truck, Dalton told Sam, "Look, take off. Get them out of here. Run through any barrier you have to."

"Addy?"

"She's already out there with Graham and the others. Just *go*. You've got the radio."

"Where are you and Rick going?"

"To Clarisse. They still have her."

Sam nodded and then floored it, heading for the main entrance. Dalton watched him as he took off; the guards didn't even try to stop him at that rate of speed. In fact, they opened the gate when they saw him coming. Not one shot was fired. *Something screwy is going on with some of these guards. They sure are making this easy.*

"Go, Sam," Dalton whispered before he ran off to meet up with Rick, who was keeping an eye on the lab where they thought Clarisse was being questioned by Harding.

47

Found Out

Clarisse sat across from Harding, who held the letter between his fingers and looked around her lab for the evidence that might prove her guilt or innocence. He hoped she wasn't capable of the crime the letter suggested.

"What can you tell me about this, Clarisse?" His words sounded scolding. She stared blankly at him or beyond him, showing no emotion on her face.

"What did you inject into them? You have to tell me. Please, Clarisse, don't play this game. I need to know."

"This"—he shook the piece of paper—,"this piece of paper says you gave them a virus that will result in the genocide of their people. Clarisse! You can't do this!" His arm swept the lab equipment from the surface of the work table in an instant, creating a cascade of glass that landed on the floor.

Clarisse flinched and stepped backward and into the soldier

guarding her in order to avoid the flying glass. The soldier braced her, one hand on her shoulder; the other hand rested on his holster.

"The prisoners are secure?" he yelled to the soldier.

"Yes, sir."

Harding strode closer, to face her. "How long?"

She stared past him.

"How long until they die? How long until they're carriers? And how long have you been planning this behind my back?"

He swung his arm around to strike her, and she braced herself, but before his hand could reach her the soldier intervened and blocked Harding with his own arm. Then Clarisse was shoved behind him and Harding was faced with his own soldier holding him at gunpoint.

"What in the hell are you doing, soldier?" Harding lunged for him.

"Don't, sir. I'm warning you." The soldier then turned to Clarisse. "You'd better run, doctor. They're waiting for you out front."

She was stunned.

With her hands still cuffed behind her back, Clarisse ran to the door, turning and smiling at Harding before she fled. *I did what I had to do*, her smile told him.

48

The Escape

Rick had retrieved their Jeep as Dalton waited and watched the doorway for any action. He could see faint shadows through the windows, but nothing more. Their plan was to storm the room, retrieve Clarisse, and then get the hell out of there. As soon as Rick had returned with their vehicle, Dalton spotted Clarisse at the door. With her hands still tied behind her back, she ran to him. Guards watched the scene unfold, but no one intervened. Dalton quickly cut away her binds and asked, "What about the rest of your supplies?"

"Did you load up our room with the laptop and chest under the bed?"

"Yes."

"Then we have everything we need. That was my duplicate stash. The rest I can replace. I always make backups. Plus, he just destroyed the vaccine and the virus when he threw a temper tantrum back there. Why are the guards helping us?"

"I don't know," Dalton said. Rick just drove them through the main gate, the guards waving good-bye. "Maybe they've had enough of living the perfect life. Maybe they want to live in reality for a time."

"What about the prisoners?" she asked.

"Sam's got them," Dalton said and then showed Clarisse his bite marks.

"She bit you? *That bitch!*"

Rick piped up, "Yeah, well, can we blame her? We had it coming, I guess. We made her a weapon."

"She doesn't know that," Clarisse said as she attended to Dalton's wounds.

"I still can't believe Reuben did this. I mean, I knew he had a hard time with some of the things we did—but this?" Dalton complained.

"Where'd they go anyway?" Clarisse asked.

Dalton shook his head. "I don't know. North, possibly? Maybe he needs to be on his own to live with his own conscience."

"Yeah, well. He's subjecting his family to it too." Dalton said.

"We can only help those who realize the reality of this world. Back there? That's not life. That's crazyville. You can't pretend your way out of this. You have to meet it head on or die trying," Rick said as he sped down the rough road out of Hope.

"How much longer before we meet up with the others at the rendezvous? And where are they?" Clarisse asked.

"About twenty minutes more. Barring any problems," Rick said. "No one's following us, right?"

Dalton looked again. "Nope, not a soul."

"We have to get the prisoners planted in the next three days. How are we going to do that?" Clarisse reminded them.

Dalton rubbed his head. "I'm not sure yet, but we'll make it happen."

The three of them fell into silence then. So much had happened in the last several minutes that they hadn't had a chance to process it yet.

Dalton, though he didn't say it, held Clarisse a little tighter. He'd heard the yelling in the lab and worried that Harding might try to harm Clarisse in his rage. She leaned into him and closed her eyes. To rest was a gift in this life, no matter how short the time. Finally, they were away from the falsely named village of Hope and were now making their way back to their own country. And they had a cure for the pestilence that infected it.

49

Fishing

Once Macy received the radio call from Graham, everything proceeded at a rapid-fire pace. She told Mark and McCann immediately, and they packed up their gear as fast as possible. Lucy gathered Addy and the younger boys and together they mounted up their supplies and made their way back to the vehicles.

Per their plan, McCann drove the horse trailer and Mark drove the truck and they headed back to the northern tip of Ross Lake, where they would cross back into the United States. It didn't take long. They drove the trucks off the main road and down into the forest to conceal their position.

The younger children were scared, but Marcy and Lucy did a good job of allaying their fears. "No, your Dad isn't dead," Macy heard her sister relay to Kade as she passed them by on her way to haul water to the horses. Macy was worried—they all were—and she hoped that what her sister had just said wasn't a lie.

"How long do we wait?" Macy asked Mark and McCann as she placed a bucket of water in front of the horse.

"I don't know. We'll have to make camp here tonight if no one shows up," Mark said.

"Someone will show. This has been the evacuation plan that we've all studied, over and over. I just hope they were able to get the food supply or it's going to be rough for a while. We have enough to last us only tonight and tomorrow, and lots of little mouths to feed," McCann said.

"Did Graham say anything else when he called in?" Mark asked.

"No, he just said, *Code evac. Now go!* I didn't ask questions. I just said okay. He sounded scared." Macy tried to keep the worry out of her voice. "I hope everyone else is okay."

McCann put an arm around her. "Graham's fine. He'll be here soon. Look, if no one shows up in the next two days, I'll go back and see what happened."

"No. You can't do that!" Mark said. "I can't take care of all these kids by myself. What if she's right? What if you don't come back? They told us never to split up like that. They said to stay together, and we're staying together." He stomped off to gather firewood.

McCann raised his eyebrows.

Macy said, "He never acts out like that."

"He's got a point," McCann said. "Let's just give it some time. Someone will show up."

BY LATE AFTERNOON they heard a truck on the roadway. Marcy jumped up. "Someone's coming!"

"Get everyone into hiding," advised McCann. "We don't know who it is."

Lucy and Marcy gathered the children and took them farther into the woods for cover, while Mark, McCann, and Macy split up and moved toward the roadway to spy on the vehicle.

Soon they could see that it was one of their own trucks, but waited further until the driver slowed down. A dark figure peered out the window for signs of people, and a baby cried in the backseat. The door of the pickup opened and Graham stepped out when a second truck pulled up behind them. The driver turned out to be Olivia.

McCann came out of hiding and approached Graham.

"Oh, man, it's good to see you!" Graham said.

"What's happening?" McCann asked as Mark and Macy also showed up.

"I almost couldn't tell you guys were here," Graham said.

"We pulled down into the trees and covered our tracks," Mark said.

Macy reached for the crying baby before Graham could soothe her and Bang climbed out, clearly relieved to have the crying baby in someone else's arms.

McCann wasn't sure if Graham was avoiding his question or if he was just rattled. "Graham, what happened?"

"Harding found out about our plans. He tried to stop us. He may have, in fact; I don't even know. Dalton had Olivia and I pack up everything and get out."

Olivia looked shaken. Bethany ran up and into her arms. "Oh, thank God." Olivia tried to hold back tears as the children gathered around her. She quickly went into mothering mode, counting the little ones.

Graham patted her on the back. "They're coming. I'm sure they'll make it, Olivia." But he wasn't sure himself, and he wasn't sure that lying to her was the right thing to do.

McCann asked, "Should we stay here and wait or go farther in?"

"I say we wait here. We have most of the supplies. We can set up a few tents. We should be fine here for the night. We'll wait and see. If they aren't here by morning, we'll make different plans."

A half hour later, Sam arrived with a truckload of prisoners.

50

Duct Tape

After driving through the gate, Sam continued to fly down the abandoned roadway. He was not only fleeing crazy town but closing the distance between him and his daughter. Though he knew she was probably fine, she was all he had left in the world, and he didn't want to have her out of his sight for any longer than was necessary. It bothered him that morning when she wanted to go fishing with the others. He'd reluctantly let her go, chiding himself for being overprotective. He knew she needed to hang out with other kids. *McCann will keep them all safe*, he had reassured himself.

His mind was jogged from his thoughts when he heard the woman in the back grunting. When he turned around, the man was doing his best to prevent her from smashing herself into Sam from behind. Even though her hands and legs were tied together she had somehow managed to wriggle free, and he guessed her intent was to cause an accident by throwing herself into him. The man in the back's face was beet red from the force she was exerting on him

Sam reluctantly pulled over, shaking his head. *This crazy bitch is relentless. No, we just had to stop and grab one of the lumps in front of the fire. Dammit!* He brought the truck to a stop, took out the keys, and got out. He made his way to the back, and the only thing he could think of to do was to use a roll of duct tape to restrain any part of her that moved. He didn't want to hurt her because of her value to their plan, but he couldn't allow her to hurt anyone else, either.

He got in the back and pushed her to the bottom of the truck bed while kneeling on her back. He taped her hands completely together so that she couldn't even move her fingers. He ran tape around her ankles and secured them—bending her knees—to her thighs. He taped her mouth shut, but left enough space so she could breathe through her nose. That would keep her menacing efforts down to focusing on her breathing. And as he would do to any spooked mare, he taped her eyes shut.

Sam sat her up and taped her arms to her back and her torso to a bar that ran the length of the truck. He looked at the boy, who cowered in the corner, thinking he was next, and the third man, who only smiled back at him. "Maybe that will keep her still for a while," Sam said. The man nodded, looking relieved to have the woman restrained properly and out of his hair for a while.

And then Sam looked back again at the young man. He was sweating and Sam thought he was probably starting to run a fever. *Hell, we've already killed them.*

Once he was back on the road it didn't take him long before he neared the entrance to their chosen hideout location. He prayed his daughter was all right; He didn't know what he'd do without her.

Once he pulled up, he leaped out of the truck. Mark and McCann were guarding the vehicles, and McCann shook his hand and, before Sam could ask, smiled and said, "She's fine. She's with the others."

There was pounding on the back of the cab which caused Mark to look at Sam with raised eyebrows that indicated a question.

"I've got the prisoners," Sam said.

"You do? Where are the others?"

Sam took a deep breath. "They should be on their way. Dalton said to go, so I did. Last I saw them, they were trying to get Clarisse out of questioning. The guards seemed to be on our side."

"What do we do with the prisoners?" Mark asked.

"I don't know. Leave them in there, I guess. It's probably safest for all of us. The boy is running a fever already. We need to get them in place. The woman keeps trying to kill us, so we need to be careful with her. The oldest one, he seems to be on our side. Hell if I know what's going on." Sam made his way to the back of the truck to see what was going on inside.

Once he opened it, everything was as it was before, only the woman had worked one of her feet free and was pounding on the flooring of the truck. Sam pulled off another length of duct tape and plastered her foot to the floor. He opened a bottle of water and gave both the boy and the man as much as they wanted. When he got to the woman, he ripped off the tape, but before he could give her the water, she spat in his face. Both Mark and McCann jumped back. Sam didn't react out of anger, he simply wiped it away and then squeezed her jaws open with one hand and poured the water into her mouth. Then he shut her mouth and pinched her nose. She struggled a bit, but she eventually swallowed the water. "You're not dying on my watch, missy. We can do it this way if you want."

"Man!" Mark said.

"Yeah, I know. She bit Dalton. She tried to choke Clarisse. Don't give me a hard time for restraining her. She's dangerous as hell."

"No, I meant the kid. He looks sick," Mark said. "He's not contagious to us, right?" He took a step back.

"No. Only if you've had their vaccine."

"I wish we didn't have to do it this way," McCann said.

"You and me both son, but this is the truth. It's brutal, it's ugly, but you both need to know that we're fighting back with the same evil that they put on us, and it's a horrible thing."

51

Guarding

It was nearly dusk by the time the last of them arrived at the hideout. Again Mark and McCann guarded the entrance after they'd moved the vehicles down into the forest, keeping the prisoners secure in one of the trucks.

There were greetings and hugs, and then remorse followed because no one could forget Tala. It felt as if they were leaving her behind. Their plan was underway, but for now, it remained a mystery as to how they would place the prisoners in the most populated areas to be as efficient as possible for their purposes.

After Dalton had set up a tent for him and Clarisse, he found her gazing into the campfire while rubbing her sore neck.

"Let me take a look at that," he said clicking on a flashlight.

"No, it's fine. I'll survive."

He shone the light around the front of her neck and décolletage anyway, despite her protests. He flicked off the light and growled, got up and walked away.

He returned shortly after retrieving an instant ice pack and two ibuprofen with a bottle of water from their medical kit. By the time Clarisse had taken the ibuprofen and drank some water, the ice pack was getting chilly. Dalton had Clarisse hold it to her neck, and he wouldn't take no for an answer. What he had seen with the flashlight made him want to go to the prisoner van and take it out on the aggressor.

"Did you pass out?"

She looked at him and smiled, trying to ease his worry. "Nearly, but not quite. The other prisoner, the older one, he stopped her. I thought it was Sam at first, but it wasn't. If it hadn't been for that man . . ." She shook her head, not knowing what might have happened.

Dalton growled again and pulled her toward him. "I'm sorry I wasn't there. I sent you to do something far too dangerous. It's my fault."

"Dalton, *all* of this is too dangerous. We still have to get them into populated areas. We still have to place them. We may die doing it, but we know it must be done."

He nodded. "You need some sleep. You're going to be pretty sore tomorrow."

He kissed Clarisse and helped her up. She went into their tent and he closed the flap so that she'd have some privacy. Then he went to find Rick and the others and warned himself to steer clear of the prisoner van. He didn't trust what he might do the woman after seeing how she nearly killed Clarisse. They needed to make plans, and they needed to make them now.

When he approached the others, Rick had just shut the prisoners up for the night after giving them food and water and a blanket each.

"The boy's definitely running a fever already. Could it be the virus so soon?" He washed and dried his hands while he talked. "The woman," he shook his head. "I felt her head, but no such luck, she seems fine. Same as the man."

"Do you think they know what they've been given?" Graham asked.

Rick shook his head, "I think the older guy does, but I'm not sure about the others."

"Well it doesn't matter," Dalton said. "Tomorrow we head back to the cabins on Ross Lake, and after that we'll need to designate the three best places to plant them."

"There were two seaplanes in a hanger back on the south end of Ross Lake—remember? Who knows how to fly?" Graham asked. "I sure don't."

"Well, I do," Dalton said. "I can take one. Rick does, and Reuben did. Clarisse also has a license, but there's no way in hell she's going. She's needed with the group. Sam, I don't suppose you fly?"

"Um . . . no." Sam said.

"What about McCann?" Dalton asked Graham.

"He's on watch. I don't think so unless he flew crop dusters, but something tells me I don't want him running this one just like you don't want Clarisse to."

Dalton agreed.

"I suppose one of us could take two of the prisoners. *If* we can find enough fuel, that is," Rick said.

"In any event, I think the cabins on the lake are a defensible place to be, and we can plan from there."

"What about the dam guy?" Graham said.

"Are we sure there is a dam guy?" Rick said.

"Yeah, I'm pretty sure the dam guy's there," Sam put in. "That didn't happen on its own."

"All right, let's get some sleep before sunup. We'll deal with that dam guy tomorrow," Dalton said, fully aware that even in these dark and tense moments the men were again having a bit of fun with wordplay.

Everyone retired to the tents as the last rays of sunlight had disappeared behind the mountains.

Graham went over to Olivia to retrieve the baby. Although she offered to keep Tehya for the night, he wanted her with him. He didn't mind waking and feeding her and peering into her eyes, as dark brown as Tala's were. He found it a comfort and, above all, he wanted the baby to know *he* was her father.

Bang followed him sleepily to his tent too and settled down with a pallet between them to keep the baby safe.

Dalton had watched as they retired to the tent. He wished more than anything that he could bring Tala back for Graham. He knew the pain: losing his own wife Kim had been excruciating, even though when she died he no longer loved her the way that Graham loved Tala. This reminded him that he'd nearly lost Clarisse today, and he found himself walking toward her before he's intended to—if anything, just to hold her and pray that he could get them all through this safe and sound.

52

Return to the Cabins

Early the next morning, they broke camp and eased back into the road leading to Ross Lake's northern shore. The barge remained where they had left it, and again they spent hours transferring the vehicles down the lake to the cabins. They thought about how best to keep the prisoners, and though Rick entertained the idea of putting them up in cabin 7, where Rueben and his family had stayed the last time, Sam argued that the escape risk was just too great and he didn't have enough duct tape left for the woman, so they would remain in the truck for now.

Graham opened the door to cabin 8, holding the baby in his arms, but without Tala by his side. It seemed lonely and quiet. Macy picked up on his melancholy and offered to take the baby for a while. He let her. As he unloaded their belongings, he found himself still in a daze. He put everything where it had once been—without Tala to tell him where it should go. *God, how I miss her.*

"Graham, Dalton's called a meeting. They want you to come by the office," Mark said.

Graham looked at Macy. "Don't worry. I've got Tehya," she said.

"She needs a bottle in a few minutes," Graham reminded her.

"It's all right—really, go ahead. I can take care of her. I'll make us some lunch too," she said.

Graham looked around at the kids, *his kids*: Macy holding the baby; Bang watching Graham, but leaning against Mark; Marcy in the kitchen, putting things away; and McCann holding the door open for him while keeping one eye on the lake for intruders.

"I'll watch them. Don't worry," McCann said.

Graham nodded. This was indeed his family now. Each of them had come to him at some point over the past year, and in such a short time they had come to depend on one another as any family would. He still hadn't figured out how he would go on without Tala, but having this family helped him, made it possible for him to draw each next breath into his ragged lungs.

"Okay, I'll be back as soon as I can."

∽

"Do you think the gas in the planes is still good?" Sam asked as Graham walked through the office doorway.

"I don't know. I guess we'll find out soon enough," Rick said.

Then Dalton and Clarisse walked into the office as well.

"This is it, guys," Dalton began when everyone was settled. "This is where we plan to save the world after the greatest crime of all time."

"I know there's not that many of us, but we're going to do what we can and hopefully when this is all over we can find others out there who not only managed to survive the pandemic but also hid from the barbarians."

"Who's flying the planes, and when are we leaving?" Rick asked, "I don't think the boy is going to last too much longer."

"I just gave him some ibuprofen to reduce his fever. That should help," Clarisse interjected.

It seemed odd to care for the people they were using as weapons. It seemed even odder to be in the situation they now found themselves in, but that was life. The only way to win now was to fight fire with fire.

Dalton unfolded a map of the United States. "To answer your question, Rick, you will take one of them, and I'll take the other two. You should be able to get there and back with a full tank. I'll have to land somewhere and find more fuel for the rest of the trip."

"Wait! There has to be another way! You can't deposit both of them on your own and make it back," Clarisse complained. She was certain this plan meant death for Dalton. Graham realized this was the closest he'd ever seen her to hysterics.

Dalton put his arm around Clarisse. "There's no other way. Rick and I are the only ones who can fly. We only have two planes. As it stands, that's the plan," he diverted his attention back to the map. "We'll leave tonight, after dark. Rick, you'll take yours over to Seattle. That's our first, best option"—he drew his finger along the map —"from our current position at Ross Lake to Lake Union in Seattle. Use your best judgment to get him close to population. Then, get your ass back here."

"I'll sedate them for the trip. It should make it easier for you to put them into place," Clarisse said, her voice still on the edge of emotion.

Rick nodded. "Anything to make it easier."

Dalton took a deep breath, "That leaves me and the other two. I'm going to head to L.A. with both of them."

"Dalton no! You'll never get out of there. That's a one-way trip!" Clarisse exclaimed.

Dalton responded quietly, "Look, there's no other way, but I have a plan. I may not even have to land in a public place. I'll find something remote, and then I'll make my way back. I'll travel by night. It will take me a while, but I *will* make it back, plus it will be a good opportunity to see if the plan is working along the way. I could even hide out for a while until I think it's safe."

Graham swallowed hard. The plan was suicide, and even he knew it. He glanced at Clarisse. Silent tears rolled down her face, her arms crossed over herself; she knew it too.

Dalton studied the map, leaning over it with both hands, "I wish we could get one of them to Denver, but we only have the two planes," he said, ignoring the emotion filling the room.

53

The Hanger

Later in the afternoon, while everyone else settled in at the cabins, Dalton, Sam, and Rick boated back to the hanger on the south end of Ross Lake that they'd discovered on their last trip to see if the planes were still in working order.

Dalton unlocked the latch on the hanger door and pushed it open; the metal clanging reverberated across the lake.

"Well, they're still here," Dalton said.

"Let me check the fuel levels," Rick said, sliding a foot over to the pontoon of the first seaplane. Sam stood guard at the door; they were still antsy over the possibility of a dam guy.

Dalton was thankful that Graham had agreed to keep watch back at the cabins. Clarisse was still upset with Dalton over his latest scheme to save the world. She had every right, he supposed, but there really was no other choice. He'd make it back to them—*he would*—and he thought he'd managed to convince Clarisse of this.

"There's some, but we've got to get more. There's a fuel station at the end of the dock. I hope there's enough for the trips we plan on taking. Let's see if we can get her started up," Rick said and continued to check out the engine.

"Okay, while you're doing that, I'll go check the fuel station and see how full it is. I noticed that there was both marine fuel and aviation fuel the last time we passed through." Rick nodded, and Dalton walked along the wooden dock as he heard the plane's engine sputter and finally kick to life. Rick decide to let it run for a while and went to check out the other plane. Dalton's footsteps ceased to be heard over the engine noise. The fuel station was located not far from the dam itself. Everything looked desolate. Though the late afternoon sun glowed still, there was a slight breeze of warm air. Kim had often commented that these conditions were *fire weather*; Dalton hoped that wasn't the case today. The closer he got to the dam building, the more the hair on his arms started to rise.

There was something about the building itself that bugged him. The last time they were here, the concrete and steel building was locked up tight. They could have blasted their way in, but there was no need to waste ammo or attract attention at the time.

Dalton stopped at the fuel tanks and checked their level. Satisfied there was enough for their needs, he stood still, enjoying the warm summer breeze. He put his hands on his hips, and chuckled a little to himself. Clarisse called this his John Wayne pose. Now, ever since she'd first said that, he couldn't do it without thinking of her smiling at him. He'd do his best to make it back to her and his boys, but if he didn't, he'd kill himself to make this mission successful. He'd do it gladly.

It was good to be back on his own turf. He'd missed it every day while they were in Canada. He felt like a traitor while they were there. He heard the next plane's engine sputter to life and then turned around when he heard a metal door screeching open from behind him. He spun on his boot heel, weapon automatically drawn, and down to one knee he flew.

"Don't shoot!" came a voice he didn't recognize.

Then, of all the shocks he could have endured right then, he never in his life expected to see Sheriff running at him, full tilt.

"Sheriff?" he held his arms wide open for the dog, who flew into him and slobbered all over him. Dalton forgot the stranger for a moment in his confusion.

When he looked up, a man stood with his arms held high above his head. He was balding and had more hair in his white mustache and beard than on his head. He stood there dressed in a neat blue plaid shirt and jeans. Dalton continued to pet Sheriff with his left hand, but kept his gun in the right.

"Who are you?"

"Dalton, you okay?" Sam yelled, and that's when Dalton realized the engine noise had stopped.

"Yeah!" he yelled back.

"Is that *Sheriff*?" Rick yelled this time, but Dalton didn't answer. Instead he waited for the stranger to say something.

"My name's James. I'm the dam superintendent," he said.

"Okay. Please don't move," Dalton said.

"I won't. I'm not armed."

Then, as Rick and Sam came up behind Dalton, they ran to Sheriff, who launched into another fit of slobbering welcome.

"I never thought we'd see him again! Wait till the kids find out!" Rick exclaimed.

"Who is *that* guy?" Sam asked suddenly.

"Is he the dam guy?" Rick asked before Dalton could answer.

"Yeah, he's the dam guy. This is James, the dam superintendent," Dalton said in a kind of trance as he stared at the guy. *Graham was right! Holy hell!*

"Where did you find him?" Dalton asked James.

The old man took a breath and motioned with his arms. "Can I put my arms down?"

"Turn around first, please," Dalton said, and the old man complied. He patted the man down and found no weapons. "Okay, you can put your arms down."

"After you guys left the last time, a few days later I followed your tracks north for a while, I found this dog, injured, along with two others. I recognized them from the surveillance cameras I have up." He nodded. "Yes, I watched you on your last trip through. I keep track of this place, and Ross Lake as well. It's my job to take care of the whole area, including Ross Dam. I keep the dam running and keep the cabins in shape. I didn't mean to scare you all that night when I turned on the power. I could see how it spooked you. Sorry about that."

"Are you susceptible to the virus?" Dalton asked.

"No, I guess not. My whole family passed. Everyone who worked here, they're all gone too," he said with a wave of his hand as if those he knew had flown away on the heated breeze.

"So you're immune, then?" Sam said.

"I suppose so but thanks for leaving the vaccine. I have them in the refrigerator."

Remembering Graham's warnings Rick asked. "Do you have a problem with us here? Using your equipment?" Rick wanted to know where on the crazy meter this guy might turn up.

"I listen to the radio. I know what's going on out there. You're the only *Americans* I've seen here in a long time. Use whatever you want."

"Have you seen the terrorists? Have they been here?" Dalton asked.

"Nope, not yet. They're in Seattle, and they're closing in on the Coulee Dam. We're small fry for now, but it won't be long," James said in a warning tone.

"What do you plan to do?" Dalton asked.

"I have a few tricks up my sleeve, but I'll go down with the ship, so to speak," he said. "What do you people plan to do?"

Dalton wasn't sure he could trust the man. "We're working on something."

"That's what I thought," he said with a grin. "If you need the planes, go ahead and take them. I have one more in a hanger to the west"—he pointed—"tucked away in the trees over there." He pointed.

"Look, James, may I shake your hand properly?" Dalton asked.

"Sure," James said, taking a few steps toward Dalton. They met in the middle. All three shook his hand, and it was more of series of embraces—acknowledgment of the living, of those who'd been through hell and continued on.

Sheriff ran over to James and he reached down and petted his head. "He's a great dog. The others are down below, but I thought you guys would recognize him first. He seems to be the alpha."

"He *is* a great dog. I know some kids who are going to really be happy to see him again," Sam said.

"How did you come about them?" Dalton asked.

"Well, I keep tabs on things around here. I knew about the tidy group up in Hope, and I assumed that's where you were headed. Then one day I decided to take a hike north to be sure you guys made it. I saw what looked like a scuffle before their roadblock. Shell casings littered the roadway. I assumed the worst. Then, I ran into this guy. He was injured. A bullet must have grazed his back flank, but he's healed well now. Two others followed him out of the woods. I keep them inside most of the time. There are wild dogs around here that will eat a man alive now, and I didn't want them falling into those packs."

Dalton felt for Sheriff's injury and found he'd healed over well.

"We, um . . . we had some trouble with the group in Canada, and we thought the dogs might be dead," Rick said.

"Well, I've got a surprise for you. Not only are they alive, but one of the others *multiplied* a few weeks ago," James said.

It was Rick that finally uttered, "What?"

"You mean Elsa?" Sam asked.

"She had nine pups," James said, "One didn't make it."

"She had eight puppies?" Dalton asked to confirm the statement.

James nodded. "Yes, and I'm pretty sure this one"—he pointed to Sheriff—"is the culprit, judging from the puppies' markings. Some are white, while others are a combination of the two. Cute little things."

Dalton's radio vibrated, and he stepped away from the group to talk to Graham on the other end while the conversation carried on behind him.

"Everything okay?" Graham asked. "Over."

"Yeah. You're never gonna guess who we met. Over."

"Who? Over."

"The dam guy."

"Dalton, do you need help? Over."

"No, it's okay. He's fine, Graham, trust me."

"Don't trust him, Dalton."

"He has Sheriff, Graham."

"He has *what*?"

"Sheriff!"

"He has *Sheriff*? Is he okay?"

"Yeah, he's great. Would Sheriff trust a bad guy?"

"No never. Oh, my God. Get him back here!"

"We will, buddy. It's okay. There are other surprises too."

"Okay, be careful, Dalton. Over."

"Always. Out."

When Dalton returned to the group, James was saying, "I'll take you guys below, if you'd like to see the pups."

"Sure, but we need to get back soon. If you don't mind, we'll take Sheriff and the others back with us. Why don't you come with us too, and then we'll make plans from there?"

He could see James was a little skittish. He was an older man and had been on his own for a long time now.

"That'd be nice. I haven't seen too many people. Only the ones dying. I couldn't believe it when I was the only one left. I've worked and lived here nearly my whole life except for stints in Vietnam and Korea.

"Then, listening to the radio, I figured out what was going on. There are some uprisings going on, scattered here and there in the country. There's a fight going on now in Texas. Some survivors are holding out, but they don't stand a chance for long. There are too many of the jihadists. I was a pilot back in Vietnam. I can help with whatever you're planning."

"Sounds like you got some good radio equipment in there. What else can you tell us?" Rick said.

The old man took a deep breath to calm himself. "It's like a cancer spreading and taking over. Those who are surviving are doing their best, but it doesn't look good. There was a group down in Virginia, probably the first one that was well organized, like you guys. They had big coordinated plans, lots of weapons, but then they were wiped out. Every last one of them. A lady was broadcasting the events taking place. It was a massacre. Whatever you're planning, I hope it works. I'd rather go down fighting than sit here on my ass listening to it all. That's why I introduced myself. I figured that since you guys had come back there must be a plan."

They were all in a mild state of shock from James's information.

"At least there are some survivors left. That means there's hope," Sam said.

"Yes, hope and a plan that we'd better get started on or we'll miss our chance," Dalton said.

James brought them below and pretty soon the grown men were reduced to coos as cuddly round balls of fur greeted them.

"You did good, Elsa," Sam said, petting her. He noticed that Frank no longer wore his splint and had only the slightest limp. He'd healed well.

Dalton could swear the dog smiled at his compliment while she enjoyed the attention.

"Gosh, Dutch would be shocked to see this," Dalton said.

Sam and Rick lowered their heads and nodded automatically to the mention of Dutch.

"He was one we lost over in the battle of Cascade, where we came from. Bravest soldier I've ever met," Dalton explained to James.

Inside the dam building, everything was neat and tidy. James showed them the radio and monitor room where he spent most of his time. Knowing James spent a lot of time locked inside, Dalton saw why the man kept busy. It was a lonely, concrete and steel tomb. Nothing about the man alarmed Dalton, though he wore the same look that they all carried, the shock of tragedy was on his face, as it was on the faces of all survivors.

"Here's a box we can use to transport the pups. I'll pack a bag for myself to stay in the cabins overnight. By the way, I noticed you guys are missing five members. Did something happen over in Hope?"

Sam and Rick let Dalton answer the question. "We lost one as she was giving birth. It was a real tragedy that none of us is over yet, nor will we ever be. Tala was amazing. And we lost a family of four due to our plans; they decided they could not live with what we are about to do on their conscience, so they took off on their own. I wish them well. I hope to hell they're going to be okay."

"Well, I can understand that. So, nothing at the hands of the people of Hope?"

"No, they're an odd bunch, and their leader is more like a dictator, but the people there are catching on. When they learned of our plans, he tried to stop us, so we escaped—but with the guards' help, so I don't think they are going to put up with his antics much longer. Sure, he's kept them alive, but that's no life."

James nodded in agreement while Rick and Sam gathered the puppies into the box. Elsa sniffed at the task, and Sam continued to pet her to calm her down. "Don't worry, mama, you're coming too."

Once on the boat, the dogs seemed used to this kind of ride and knew what was happening. "I take them around with me on my rounds," James explained. "They're great dogs."

"We can't thank you enough for taking care of them," Dalton said.

As they got underway, James pointed out the other hanger where the extra plane was kept, and said it was in complete working order. He ran all the planes every now and then to keep the engines in good repair.

Once they were near the dock, they spotted McCann, Macy, and Graham; an eager Sheriff jumped out of the boat and swam the rest of the way when he spotted them.

"Sheriff!" screamed Macy. She was reduced to tears in an instant. The rest of the group all came out and couldn't believe their luck at reuniting with the dogs, marveling at the bonus puppies. It was the best form of morale booster any of them could have hoped for.

Clarisse and McCann immediately checked Elsa and the puppies. They were all healthy, and when asked what he'd been feeding them, James admitted sheepishly to feeding them cooked chicken and rice most days although Sheriff often hunted for them too.

"That's the way to spoil a dog," McCann said.

"Well, let's leave the dogs to the experts," Dalton said, gathering the men in the office that was now their headquarters.

"Graham, this is James, the dam guy," Dalton said, wondering for a minute whether Graham was going to shake the man's hand. Graham looked into James's eyes as if he was studying him for something. Tentatively he shook James's hand, but he still seemed wary. Dalton figured trust would come in time—but they didn't have much time left. If any of them made it back, they would get to know each other better.

In his own mind, Dalton wasn't certain any of them would make the return trip. He would die trying, but if it meant the survival of the rest of them, so be it. There was a lump forming in his throat and the closer they got to leaving the harder it was, yet he was determined, and James's news about the state of their country made him realize they had to move now and, even so, they might be too late.

54

The Plan

"How far can this plane go in one trip fueled up?" Rick asked James.

"About 300 miles. She's in peak condition. That would mean a half hour reserve for landing leeway."

Dalton blew out a frustrated breath.

"Why? You need to go farther on one trip?" James asked.

"Yeah," Dalton pointed to the map. "We need to make it to the most populated areas, including Los Angeles. To drop off some, um .. . *cargo*. We have three subjects who are carrying the flu that will be detrimental to our enemies."

James put a hand up. "Wait a minute."

Dalton was afraid he'd said too much for a second.

"You've infected three individuals with a virus that will infect everyone?" James asked, clearly a little nervous.

Clarisse spoke up, "Ah, actually, we've developed a highly viru-lent, selective virus that adheres to the markers of a vaccine *they* received. It will only infect the enemies that have received their own vaccine."

They all stood silent while the news sunk into their new ally, hoping that he would indeed remain an ally.

"You say you've created a bioweapon, and you've infected three individuals with it to plant in the most populated areas? Do I have this correct?"

"Yes," Dalton said. "We captured three of the jihadists, and they've received the virus; they are indeed virulent bioweapons."

James was quiet for another minute, and Dalton was beginning to get nervous.

"This might work," James said, and everyone relaxed a little. "I don't mind telling you, I've listened to a lot of plotting and planning, and all of it has failed. There are so many of them, and there is no humanity in this enemy, son. There's no low too low. Terrorism is what they know. But your plan might work, and I pray that it does. I can see why your buddy had a hard time with it. He wasn't strong enough to handle the guilt of it all, but this is how it needs to be to survive. I'm in. I'm your third pilot. You say you need to go farther. My suggestion would be to take the plane to L.A. with extra fuel loaded. I've got a couple of extra bladder tanks. Know what those are?"

Dalton didn't, but he sure wanted to.

"They're called Turtle Buddies, and they're made of heavy-duty collapsible polyurethane. It's like having an extra tank of fuel that sits in your passenger seat," James said.

"That's the best news so far," Rick said, feeling hopeful.

"How many do you have?" Dalton asked, already calculating distances in his head.

"I have five but, you'd only need two to reach L.A.," James answered.

"If you're in, we're also going to Denver with the third plane," Dalton said, and James agreed with a handshake.

"If the tank sits on the seat, what do you do with the subjects?" Graham asked.

"Put them in the backseat or cargo area as the case may be. After all, it's not a joyride for them," James offered.

"We have to get them there alive and breathing. Preferably, breathing well and for an extended period of time," Clarisse said.

The remainder of the afternoon and evening were filled with planning. After nightfall, they'd start on the perilous mission. No one knew, if they'd ever set eyes on their pilots again, but still they hoped these wouldn't be one-way trips.

55

Saying Good-bye

In the evening Dalton met in his cabin with his sons Kade and Hunter. The little boys were covered in dog hair and sweat, and they didn't understand why their dad wanted to talk to them alone, though they knew something had to be going on due to all the excitement around the cabins. This was the part Dalton dreaded the most. If he admitted the truth to himself, he knew he might never see his sons again, and this meeting would be etched in their memories forever. They would forever recall the words he was about to say.

Dalton put Kade on his knee as he sat in a comfortable chair, with Hunter leaning against him. They were just little boys. It killed him, knowing what he must do next, which was to break their hearts, but hopefully it meant their survival for years to come.

"Dad, what are you doing with those airplanes out there? Are we going to fly somewhere?" Hunter asked.

Kade looked excited and looked up to him for the answer.

"Um . . . well, I'm going to go on a little trip tonight. That's why we have the planes out front. We're getting them ready to go."

"Are *we* going?" Kade asked.

"Actually, you are going to stay here with Clarisse and Graham and the others. I'll be gone for a little while. That's what I wanted to tell you guys."

"When will you be back?" Kade asked.

"He's *not coming* back," Hunter said, pulling away from his father, but Dalton caught his arm before he could get away.

He stared into his son's eyes and knew he couldn't lie. "Hunter, look at me," he said, giving him a gentle shake. The boy looked up at him on the verge of tears. "This is a very important trip. We have a way to get rid of the bad guys. I'm going to try—I swear to God, I will do my damnedest to get back to you. But if I don't do this"—his voice was cracking now as he shook his head and tried to form the words—"no one will live for long. Not you, not Clarisse, not even Addy or Bethany. I *have* to do this. Do you understand, son?"

Hunter cried, and Dalton thought perhaps he'd gone too far. It was so hard not to shatter their world, and he had no idea how to go about conveying this life-or-death matter to them so that if he didn't return it would mean they would at least remember that he loved them and that he'd gone on this mission as a last effort to save them.

He pulled Hunter in close and cried as he hugged his sons. Soon Clarisse came in, having heard every word. When he saw her, he pulled her in too and they stayed that way for a long while before Dalton pulled himself away, determined to save them all no matter the cost.

56

Departure

The engines sputtered to life. Rick took off, waving a last good-bye to Olivia while she wept openly on the dock, Bethany at her side. It was torture. Off he flew, his lights turned off to avoid being seen. If all went well, he'd be back by dawn.

Next was James. His last words were to Sheriff as he knelt down to the dog's level and hugged him: "Good-bye, old boy."

He waved to Graham, having earlier told him how to handle the spillway of Diablo Dam if he never made it back. He'd told him a great many things, and Graham hoped he'd be able to remember all of them. It was as if the man never intended to return, but Graham made sure to tell him he'd maintain everything until he did. Then, James took off and, after his expert lift from Lake Ross, headed toward Denver with a heavy load.

Last to go was Dalton, who hugged his cousin Mark, and then Graham. He, too, had earlier filled Graham in on a few details about hidden bunker stashes. Graham agreed that he'd take care of his sons, and Dalton remarked that he'd never worry about them under his care. He moved on to McCann and the rest before he came to Clarisse. "It's going to be fine. It's about a thousand nautical miles, which will take over nine hours, so I better get a move on while I can travel under cover of darkness." More caring and adequate words were lost to him except to say that he loved her like no other and that, no matter what, he would do everything he could to make sure he made it back to her.

She shocked him then. She leaned into his side and whispered a revelation into his ear, "I'm two weeks pregnant, Dalton. I'll carry you with me always. *I . . . love . . . you. Please* return."

Clarisse was always calculating, and she'd made sure to preserve something of Dalton within her because she doubted that their plan would preserve them all. She knew the risks. She loved him so much that she'd made it possible to have something of the both of them to never let go of.

Dalton could only hold her a moment more, stunned with the surprise news. "I love you," was what he said at last. He climbed into the cockpit, shut the door, and strapped himself in. Soon he'd left the lake and when he circled around, he looked back at them once. Though barely visible, they were all there, and he assumed they were waving. He looked ahead and gained altitude, and they were soon out of sight as he flew south toward Los Angeles and the enemy.

57

Rick's Mission

It was decided early on that Rick would take the easiest mission. Planting his virulent weapon as close to a public area in Seattle and returning home posed a dangerous mission in itself, but Rick was up for the task.

He would have taken any of the missions Dalton wanted him to, but taking this one made his chances of return better. At first he felt guilty, but one look at his wife and daughter made him think otherwise. They needed him alive and with them.

"How you doing back there?" he asked his cargo, even though the kid was unconscious.

Rick liked James, and thought it would be best to match him with the least worrisome of the jihadist prisoners, so they gave him the man who seemed compliant in their scheme.

The prisoner seemed resigned to his fate and even willing went along out of what they assumed was remorse. Instead of sedating him, they decided to keep him conscious so that the old man wouldn't have to struggle with his weight. They kept him restrained, however; when it came down to it they didn't want to give the guy free access to James if he changed his alliance again.

The kid prisoner that Rick took was strapped in the backseat. Rick looked at him through his mirror, and could see beads of sweat cascading off his face. The kid was fading fast. "Sorry buddy," Rick said, again realizing that the kid couldn't hear him, but he felt a need to say it anyway.

Rick hoped to land silently, as he'd done many times before, and then get the kid into a public area. They were each dressed in what the terrorists typically wore, and he hoped the night would further camouflage his efforts.

Forty minutes into the flight, he came to the designated area; Lake Union, which was surrounded by a park in central Seattle. It was hard to see at night, so Rick flipped down the night vision goggles he brought along for the ride. There were a few boats in the way, and some of them were floating at odd angles. He circled around and got into a path to land unencumbered by the stray boats. He saw no one out in the night, and with any luck he'd get the boy into place and get the hell out of there within a few minutes.

The plan was simple. He landed, quickly got out of his harness, popped the door open and tossed out a dingy that autoinflated. As he picked up the boy, Rick could feel the fever through his clothing. "I'm sorry kid," he said as he placed him into the dingy. He gave him a water bottle and cut off the restraints on his hands and ankles. He pushed him toward shore with his foot, and watched as the dinghy floated away. He saw a few flashlights pop on in the distance.

He closed the door, belted himself again, and took off. As he did another light shone toward his plane, blinding him slightly with the NVGs on. Rick flipped them up and sped away, quickly gaining altitude. He prayed no one would fire on him or the kid.

After several minutes, with the engine noise taking up his thoughts, Rick continued to push forward and watched his tail the entire time. He had fuel to spare, so he took a more easterly route to throw anyone off his intended route if he were followed.

Forty-five minutes later, he began his descent to Ross Lake. Graham held up two flashlights to help guide him in after Rick had radioed ahead.

"Welcome back, man," McCann said as Rick climbed out and McCann tied the lines to the dock. Then Olivia ran into Rick's arms. "I'm okay. It was easy in and easy out. No problems," he said with a grin.

"I hope the same goes for the other two," Graham said. Suddenly they were all grim, knowing there was little chance of that.

"Let's get rid of the plane in case they send out a search," Graham said.

Rick nodded. His heart was still beating a mile a minute. "That's thinking ahead," Rick said. "I hadn't even considered it." He climbed back into the cockpit and flew the plane over to the original hanger. McCann followed him in a smaller boat for the return ride.

Graham and Olivia waited in the office to monitor the radios while Rick and McCann stashed the plane.

"Where's Sam?" Rick asked when he got back.

"He took one of the horses and is checking the perimeter. Everyone's a little antsy tonight," Graham said.

"I can see why," Rick said. He, too, couldn't settle down.

"I'll go relieve Mark," McCann said, slipping off into the night with Sheriff in tow.

After a period of silence, Graham said, "You two should go get some sleep. You can take over in the morning, Rick."

"Yeah, you're right. We should try to sleep. It's just going to be us, a smaller crew. We all need to watch that we each get enough sleep, because we're going to be watching our backs for a while."

Graham watched the married couple leave and felt pangs. It wasn't that he was jealous, just that he missed Tala. He wanted to tell her about what they'd just accomplished, but he'd never be able to. He'd like to think she already knew, but then that would be trying to convince himself of things he didn't believe in.

What was really on his mind now was Dalton. Graham couldn't shake the feeling that he'd never see him again. His last radio transmission had been normal, a thumbs-up. They probably wouldn't hear from him again even if and when he completed the mission. The same went for James. From now on, every time he looked at Clarisse, he'd realize that she too was feeling the same thing he was. It would never end, the heartache of loss. He pictured for the first time the dead man he'd discovered at the supply house after this all began, swinging from a noose in his garage after his family had died. Perhaps it was a privilege, after all, to have taken your own life and not submitted yourself to the fight they were in now. He suddenly envied the man.

58

Dalton's Mission

Dalton knew his flight down the coast to California would be a long, daunting challenge. The single-engine Cessna 206 Stationair was up to the task, and given the auxiliary fuel tank, he figured he would have just enough fuel to make the journey. The C206 was a very capable airplane for its class, but the large floats created substantial drag; its cruise speed was around 120 knots, and the plane burned roughly eighteen gallons of fuel per hour.

Although a straight line would be the shortest, choosing that route would force him to cross several mountain ranges in the dark, which would require supplemental oxygen at those altitudes. The substantial drag created by the floats would also hinder his high-altitude performance—not to mention the potential weather hazards created by the moist Pacific air being forced upslope by the southwestern winds; icing conditions and floats simply did not mix.

With this in mind, Dalton opted for a slightly longer but safer route down the coastline. With luck, the moonlight would allow him to visually follow the coast all the way down to California, staying just far enough out to sea to remain out of sight and sound to those who might be watching from shore.

He tried not to let it get in the way, but Dalton couldn't help but think about what Clarisse had just revealed to him. Now, more than ever, he knew he had to get back to them or die trying.

Not having had the chance to be adequately rested for the journey, the near pitch black darkness and the steady drone of the airplane's engine had Dalton fighting to stay awake. *Wake up!* he said to himself, smacking a hand across his face. He checked the clock on the instrument panel. "Dammit, it's only been four hours?" he said aloud. "This is gonna be a long night."

He looked back at the unconscious prisoner, in restraints and strapped to her seat. "Fun, huh?" he asked, knowing she couldn't respond. Clarisse had made sure she was completely out for the trip. "Bet you never took a plane ride like this before. I'd love to toss you out right here, but *you* are going to serve a purpose after all, you annoying wench."

Looking to his left and realizing that the light of the moon was not illuminating the shoreline as it had been, Dalton turned his attention to the darkness up ahead. *I didn't realize just how damn hard it would be to see the coast with no city lights*, he thought. *It's like vertigo out here sometimes.* The view of the shoreline faded away into the darkness as he found himself entering an area of low visibility. Being an experienced instrument-rated pilot, Dalton was up to the task, but without ground-based navigation facilities transmitting their signals as they would have done in the days before the world collapsed, he had no way to continue to navigate adequately without a visual reference to the shoreline.

Checking the standby compass heading, Dalton adjusted his directional gyro and maintained his last heading and altitude. "We'll probably fly right back out of it in a minute," he said, looking back at his prisoner. "Like you care," he said with a chuckle. "You want to die for Allah anyway."

After some time had passed, Dalton became unnerved that he was still flying blind inside what had started out as offshore mist but was now a full-fledged cloud bank. Checking the outside air temperature, he thought, *a few more degrees and we'll be in icing conditions. With no de-ice boots on this old bird, we could be screwed. Hell, for all I know I've been steadily drifting off course and heading farther and farther out to sea.*

Checking his standby compass against his directional gyro again, he realized the gyro had precessed approximately ten degrees, leading him to drift off course. Correcting his heading back to the left, Dalton struggled to see the shoreline through his left window, but he couldn't see a thing.

Out of frustration he punched the glare shield and shouted, "Dammit! I don't have enough fuel to be messing around getting lost. This freaking cloud layer could go on for a hundred miles, for all I know. Screw it!" he said as he began a gentle descent. "Maybe we can pop out of the bottom of it. This crap probably doesn't go all the way down to the water."

Dalton descended out of his cruise altitude of five thousand feet with a shallow rate of descent while focusing intently on his instruments, only occasionally glancing outside. *Through four thousand*, he said to himself as he watched the thousands hand of the altimeter swing past 4 in a counterclockwise motion. *Still nothing. Can't see a damn thing. Thirty-five hundred. Still nothing. Three thousand. Still nothing. Shit!*

His descent passed two thousand feet and approached one thousand. *All right, that's it. I can't keep dropping till I hit the damn water. I'm making a turn toward the shoreline. I need to see something, and soon. I've completely lost track of my bearings.*

Turning twenty degrees to his left, he knew this new heading would eventually intercept the shoreline; by his own estimates he had only been drifting off course ten degrees to the right. Stopping his descent at a thousand feet, Dalton strained his eyes in an attempt to see anything at all out the windows. After a few minutes, his frustrations began to get the best of him. *Dammit! Surely I didn't drift that far off.* "Shit!" he exclaimed, aggressively shoving the control wheel to the right, narrowly avoiding a cell phone tower when his surroundings began to slowly come back into view as he exited the cloud bank.

With his pulse racing from the near miss, he pushed the throttle forward and began a climb back away from the terrain while keeping it in sight. Looking back to his prisoner, he said, "Sorry about that, sweetie. That was a close one."

"Okay. Game face!" he said to coax himself back into the proper mind-set. Scanning his instruments he thought, *The main tanks are down to fumes. I've stretched them as far as I could. Time to switch to the ferry tank.*

Reaching over to the makeshift fuel selector they had rigged up in the floor next to him, Dalton flicked on the auxiliary fuel boost pump in an attempt to maintain fuel pressure during the swap, then turned the valve. *So far so good*, he thought to himself, staring at the gauges. Then the fuel pressure suddenly dropped, causing the engine to stutter.

"Dammit!"

As he reached down to ensure that the fuel selector valve was rotated properly, the engine went silent, the propeller now only windmilling as the airspeed began to bleed off from the loss of power. Dalton immediately pitched the nose down slightly to maintain airspeed and avoid a stall while he worked the valve with his free hand.

With a pop and a shudder, the engine coughed itself back to life. The gauges all returned to their normal operating ranges as Dalton added power to recover his lost altitude. "I guess I should have tried that valve on the ground first," he said with a chuckle.

THEN, before he knew it, Dalton approached his target, only to realize the place was swarming with what looked to be military vehicles. He circled back, deciding that before he attracted their attention he should land somewhere quickly. He kept to the coast and soon found the right spot.

Once in position and seeing no one around, Dalton brought the plane in. Landing on the ocean waves was rough, but not as bad as he thought it might be. He landed south of Topanga Beach and inflated the raft. Hoisting his prisoner into it, he said, "Come on darlin'; time for you to meet up with some old friends." Then he put on his survival pack and rowed them to shore after disabling the plane and setting it to drift out to sea.

Dalton realized he only had about an hour to get the woman into a public position and get the hell out of there before the light of dawn. He looped the gagged, restrained, and unconscious body over his shoulders and ran up the beach.

He hoped he had picked the right spot, because this was his only chance. He saw what looked like an abandoned restaurant and a parking lot and headed that way. Once his feet hit the asphalt of the parking lot, he looked around. The place looked deserted. There were cars parked all over the roadway. He looked north and only saw a cliff of rocks; above that, a residential neighborhood.

"Great!" he said in frustration and out of breath. He needed to get her into a populated area. He eyed one of the cars left abandoned and headed for it. He opened the backseat and unceremoniously dumped her inside.

He checked her restraints and they were secure; the last thing he needed was to deal with her tricks, and he knew the drug would wear off soon. He felt around for keys, but there were none. Luckily he knew how to strip wires with his teeth and cross the exact two that would make the engine start.

In no time they were traveling down the Pacific Coast Highway. He couldn't believe his eyes at the devastation he saw. Whole neighborhoods were blocked off and burned to a crisp. Dead, decaying bodies littered the streets. Their deaths had to be from something other than the pandemic because by now, those bodies would be skeletons. These were hold-out carriers struck down by the terrorists.

He continued on and passed Will Rogers Beach, a few roadblocks, and more bodies along the roadsides. The night was dark, and he drove on without headlights, his NVGs firmly in place. He just needed to get her closer to where he suspected they were bringing in more personnel, and that meant closer to Los Angeles International Airport.

He'd be able to leave her there with the confidence that he'd gotten her as close as he could to their enemy and to do the most harm. But when he neared Santa Monica, it occurred to him that this was the closest he might be able to get. The roadway ahead was blocked off.

This is where they've taken up residence. Perfect.

He stopped there, just out of sight in the dark. He pulled the woman out of the back and sat her up in the front seat. He had to draw attention to her, so he turned up the radio, which was playing something in Arabic—a mundane speech, not remotely entertaining. He then ran off, climbed a wooden embankment, and headed into the night with nothing other than his survival pack. He hoped it would be enough for him to make his way home—or die trying.

Dawn light began to spill over the horizon. He turned one last time to view his handiwork as he reached the top of the embankment and glanced at the coming dawn. He saw men coming, and watched from his hidden location as one soldier approached the car, armed, and yelled to another guard. He hoped the words said in Arabic were something indicating the woman was drunk or somehow incapacitated. They guy lowered his weapon and felt for her pulse. Then he yelled for the other guy to come help, and they carried her out of the vehicle. *Bingo, two more infected. Let the death begin!* he thought when he heard a shot fired in his direction.

59

James's Mission

After a few close calls of his own and a tough time traversing the Rockies, James edged close to Denver. Having thought a lot about the plan on the way, he now tweaked it a little to gain his best advantage. He was familiar with the Denver area; his daughter had met and married a fellow from there. He and his deceased wife had visited her there on many occasions before the world failed them all.

He aimed not toward his original destination, but straight for Denver International Airport, which he knew from radio communications had been taken over by the terrorists.

A radio call interrupted his thoughts, in a language he didn't care to understand, but instead of answering, James flipped the switch off. He'd prepared himself for death. He knew it would happen, and now he intended for it to happen *this way*. It was the only thing he *could* control. His only concern was to save the life of the fellow in the cargo area. He wanted to make sure Omar lived at least long enough to infect a few of the others.

James circled around the airport, and though the runway was cluttered with military vehicles, he knew he could land even in a leveled grassy area. He lowered the plane and attempted a landing just past an army truck that had been set ablaze. It was a bumpy landing swerving at the last minute to avoid another flaming truck. Whatever was going on here had all the signs of utter chaos. Guns fired in the distance. There was fighting still going on, perhaps a resistance. He heard more shots and could tell they were getting closer. He quickly sprung himself out of the cockpit, grabbed his backpack, and then went to open the cargo area.

Omar was awake and seemed oddly contented. He had apparently resigned himself to his fate and had willingly cooperated out of what they all had assumed was remorse.

James helped him out and cut his restraints. He knew his prisoner was complicit in this plan, but even so, he didn't completely trust him. James and Omar scanned the wrecked airport, and when they saw soldiers running their way, they weren't sure what to do. Omar recognized them as his own people, and without warning, he pulled James's weapon out of his holster and drew it on James. He gave him a reassuring look, but James already knew he was a dead man. This was the best plan he could have made, however: there were five terrorists running their way, and they slowed as they approached him, shouting words he didn't understand. Omar shouted something back and nudged James to start walking.

One of the terrorists began arguing with the others, pointing at the airplane. Then more shots rang out from behind them, and everyone ducked. Soon they were following the terrorists toward a portion of the burned-out terminal.

Omar stopped for a second as the terrorists continued on and wiped his sweating brow; James could tell he now had the fever too. Omar stared into James's eyes and nodded back toward the plane. James had less than half an hour of fuel left; it was barely enough to get out of there, and he had no idea where he might land before he ran out of fuel.

Again, Omar hurriedly glanced at the plane and pushed James to go. James nodded. He'd done his duty, Omar would do the rest. He'd have to trust him. James watched as Omar wiped the fevered sweat from his forehead and smiled at him. He nodded again and James took off as fast as he could run. Shots rang out. Omar covered him as best he could, only pretending to shoot at James as he fled.

I might just make it out of here, James thought. He had no idea how he'd made it back into the plane and got it going, but now he was set to take off. Shots were fired upon him again, bullets pinging off the metal. When he looked back, it was a war not unlike he'd seen in Vietnam many years ago, with everything on fire and a land you felt that hell had given birth to. But this was his own country. He only hoped the virus worked. Almost a half hour later, as James searched for a level landing area, he spotted a convoy of military vehicles on the highway below. The last truck pulled what looked like shrouded human beings behind it, each tethered to the truck by ropes. Someone fired upon James as he swooped down for a closer look. James turned the plane around and aimed for the front of the convoy, away from the prisoners. In the end, James took out four of the five military vehicles in a fiery but effective crash. The prisoners behind the final vehicle escaped, though James didn't live to see it.

60

Anticipation

The next day, Graham woke up with Tehya squirming on his chest. He'd fallen asleep with her after his watch when he'd found Macy carrying the baby in the middle of the night, pacing back and forth in their cabin. He'd sent Macy off to bed and taken the baby into his arms. Two hours later Tehya was awake and wanting to be fed.

"Good morning," he cooed to her. After he fed her, he handed her off to Olivia and walked to the office, accompanied by Sheriff. Sam's eyes were bloodshot as he sipped a cup of coffee and monitored the radios.

"Good morning," Graham said. "What time is it, anyway?"

"After ten, but it doesn't really matter on days like this. We live around the clock," Sam said.

Graham was trying to avoid the question, but he had to ask it. "Any news?"

Sam shook his head. "No, nothing so far. I don't expect we'll hear anything from either of them for a few days. If they made it, that is."

"Yeah," Graham agreed. "How's Clarisse?"

"I saw her this morning with the boys at breakfast. She looks pretty torn up. She hasn't asked about Dalton. But I doubt she slept much last night."

"It's too early. She knows that. If Dalton makes it back, it'll be by foot or vehicle. Unless he can get his hands on another plane, but that's unlikely. Truthfully, it could be months before either one of them makes it back," Graham said.

"*If* they make it back," Sam said. "We really need to think about that possibility."

Graham took a deep breath. "Look, we're more in jeopardy now than at any time before. We need to keep our eyes open. If the terrorists figure this out and have enough time to get to us, we could be in for some real trouble. It's too early for any news of illness to come in. The only way we're going to know if it worked, will be the lack of chatter in next few days and weeks to come."

"Agreed. Look, I hate to bring it up, but it's late summer now, and we don't have enough food to get us through winter; we lost too much over the past couple of months. We should probably get to a few of those bunkers and get the MREs to stash in the dam building. We might consider living in there when winter sets in. We should think about how best to maintain our group through the colder months.

"And we need to refocus these guys. Everyone's rattled. I watched Mark this morning, peering up into the sky. They're all doing that. They're distracted. It's only the four of us leading this group now, and we need to think ahead."

Graham appreciated Sam's practical advice. They were all wrapped up waiting for the results of the plan and hoping that their comrades made it back home. But Sam was right: the winter ahead could end up being the real killer in all of this.

"Yeah, I know we're spread thin, but we have to continue to monitor the radios and keep a look out. Add to that hunting and getting supplies in. I say Rick and his family should just move into the office; he knows the radios best. You work on hunting and food supply with McCann and Macy; I'll keep up security with Mark and Marcy. We can switch off every now and then, but you're right, winter and starvation are just as dangerous as the terrorists."

"What about Clarisse?" Sam said.

"Let's give her some time. She'll fill in wherever she wants, and she's our medical officer; let's not forget that."

Sam nodded in agreement.

Just then, Clarisse appeared in the doorway with Rick.

"Hello," Clarisse said weakly.

They were all nervous. Clarisse's hair was drawn back in a tight, neat bun, but her face was pale and dark circles lined her eyes. Graham had never seen her looking this poorly.

"Have you eaten, Clarisse?" he asked.

She glanced at him, "Yeah, but I'm just not that hungry right now. I came to say I know they might not make it. It's a hard reality, but it's something we need to consider." Her lips trembled.

"We know, Clarisse," Graham said, reaching for her. She didn't cry, but let him hold her. "We're here for you. I'm sorry it had to be this way. Let us know if there is anything we can do."

She nodded her head. "We just have to keep going on," she said. "We don't have the luxury to grieve or the kids might not make it." She smiled, but tears ran down her face. She brushed them away. "And, it's for them that we need to push forward, or we've all failed. Every sacrifice we've made will be for nothing if we don't help them survive this."

61

Radio Talk

Two weeks later Rick woke early to a glorious pink and blue sunrise over the lake with wisps of clouds foretelling the coming autumn. Every day, the air that blew across the lake was a little cooler.

The radio produced nothing more than static; the last transmission had been detected a few days ago. They could only assume the virus was working. Even so, this genocide was something the adults would have to carry in their souls forever, not something to be celebrated.

They'd agreed to wait until after winter to venture out. For now, they'd hide and continue on waiting and hoping that both James and Dalton returned.

Rick poured himself some coffee. Early on, as each of the members of the group woke, or passed the office on their way to bed, they'd stop and ask the question he'd come to hate: *Any word?* Now he thought it was perhaps more sad that when he looked out the window Mark or one of the others would walk by without even asking. They were beginning to assume the worst.

"Come on, Dalton," Rick said under his breath. He sat down and turned up the radio, taking a sip of his coffee and watching out the window. McCann showed Kade how to cast a line out into the lake with Frank, the dog, watching his every move. The little boy had taken a liking to McCann and followed him everywhere. And everywhere Kade went, so too did Frank. It was funny how that happened. It seemed the dogs had their favorites.

Rick began to chuckle at the scene as Frank peered off the dock looking at what he guessed was a squirming fish on the line. That was when Rick heard something unusual within the static. He sat down his coffee harder than he meant to, and it splashed onto the counter as he fumbled with the radio knob. He turned up the receiver and tried to see if it came in again. *Maybe I'm hearing things.* A few seconds later, it happened again. It was faint and staticky. "Hey, is there anyone out there?"

62

A Realization

Clarisse woke and rushed to the bathroom again. The morning sickness seemed to skip days now, but she wasn't so lucky on this particular morning. After she cleaned up, she peeked into the boy's room and found them still asleep; the dawn's rays just entering their room were interrupted by shadows from clouds threatening snowfall. A soft glow gleamed over their small bodies.

Kade was doing well, considering; he'd stopped asking about his father in the past few weeks, but Hunter was resentful and angry. Clarisse was doing everything she could to bring him peace, but it was hard to do when she herself felt alone and scared.

There was hope, though. Survivors were gathering together. They were calling into the radio station with reports. News was spreading about a mass dying off of the terrorists due to a mystery virus.

Someone reported that an airplane took out an entire convoy of terrorists about two months ago, saving fifty Americans in the Denver area. They all speculated that it might have been James, but there was no real way of knowing.

After a long discussion, they'd decided to keep the knowledge of what they'd done to themselves, so other survivors thought the new virus a mystery. Some of them turned to religion's salvation for answers; others didn't care much focusing instead on rebuilding and locating more survivors.

They'd hung around the radio for days when the news first started pouring in. Some stations had tried posting news for survivors to locate family members, but it was quickly learned that there were few matches and that effort waned. Rick had posted inquiries into Dalton's and James's whereabouts, but so far nothing had come in.

Mostly, people just wanted to talk, to tell their tales. Though everyone had a different story, no one had a monopoly on the terror. They were all in the same position; they were all survivors.

Clarisse began issuing notices about healthcare, and Rick posted winter preparedness warnings. Soon survivors were asking them questions over the radio every day, so Rick began fielding survival questions and people made plans to meet up in the spring.

They were losing hope of ever hearing from Dalton again and had assumed the worst. Even so, Rick planned to track them come spring.

Clarisse ran her hand over her belly. She was too early to show, but several of the other camp members had already guessed. She was glad she at least had a part of Dalton within her to carry on. She never regretted her decision, even though she felt a little guilty for not telling Dalton earlier.

ONE DAY CLARISSE heard a strange sound disturbing the everyday peace of the lake. When she looked out the window, McCann was rushing Kade in front of him and getting ready to draw his gun as a speed boat was headed their way. Clarisse ran outside onto the dock to retrieve Kade when the boat slowed. Out stumbled a thin, bearded man with one arm in a sling. McCann took aim as the stranger rushed him on the deck.

Clarisse screamed, "No! Don't shoot!" He was almost unrecognizable, but she knew this ragged man was Dalton.

A shot rang out. At the last second, McCann had diverted his aim. The commotion caused everyone to run outside. Dalton collapsed onto the deck, and Clarisse ran to him. Everyone else gave them a few moments alone before they swarmed Dalton.

Against all odds he had done as he had promised; he had returned.

63

Back Home

One year later, Graham pulled the truck to a stop. It had been a long drive. He'd come from the new settlement east of Spokane. They'd gathered there with many other survivors from around the area and lived there for the last six months after the winter was over. But Graham couldn't take the growing population; he couldn't get used to the crowds, and always found himself trying to find a quiet place. He'd turned down any leadership position offered him; he didn't want to start a community, or forge a new frontier. He only wanted to raise his daughter and Bang and keep track of the other kids.

He eventually decided to go home for a while and be in peace. So after letting the older kids know his plans, he took the truck and supplies. Graham gave Bang the option of staying with McCann and Macy, but the boy chose to go with Graham instead. The others promised they would come soon too.

"We're here," he announced as he pulled Tehya from her car seat.

She was drowsy from the long journey and rubbed at her big brown eyes.

They stood there for a while gazing at the cabin, Graham holding Tehya on his hip and Bang standing at his side.

"It looks smaller than I remember," Bang said after he exited the truck with Scout, one of Sheriff's pups.

"It'll take some work to get it back into shape." Scout ran ahead through the tall grass to the cabin steps and sniffed around; so like her father once did.

Graham imagined Tala standing on the porch, like the day he'd first kissed her with snowflakes in her ebony hair. He felt her spirit here, and he wanted their daughter to feel it too.

"I miss Ennis," Bang whispered. "I remember how we fished together—down the trail." He pointed in the general direction, the trail now long overgrown.

"Yeah, there are a lot of memories here, now," Graham said as he adjusted his daughter's position on his hip and then they headed into the cabin.

Later that day, after they'd swept all the cobwebs out of the bunkroom and cleaned up the cabin, they heard a knock on the door. Graham answered it, and when Dalton and Clarisse stepped inside, Tehya toddled into Dalton's outstretched arms. "You guys all settled in? Where's Sheriff?" Dalton asked Graham.

"Yeah, I think so, Graham said. "The kids and Sheriff are coming in tomorrow. Isn't it funny? We could live anywhere, but this is our home now. We're all drawn back here. You guys returned to your spot, and we returned here."

Dalton shook his head. "I saw enough of what was out there on my trek home. They nearly destroyed it all. Maybe one day it will be livable, but for now, this is where I want to be." He hugged Clarisse to his side. "Sam and Addy, Rick and Olivia; they're all back."

Clarisse smiled up at him. "We knew you'd come back soon too. We've all become more independent and defensive. I don't think our previous trusting ways as a society will return for many generations."

Graham reached for the baby she held in her arms, and she

handed him to her. "Man, three boys!" Graham's eyes widened as he cuddled the little boy in his arms. Even as an infant, he was stocky and strong like his father. Graham looked at Clarisse. "You did good," he said. She was crying, but she smiled at him.

"What is it?" Graham asked.

"I just wish Tala were here too," Clarisse said.

Graham hugged her, "She *is* Clarisse. *This* is where she is."

AFTERWORD

A Note to My Fans

I can't tell you what an amazing journey this has been for me. Graham's Resolution is my first series, and it's bittersweet as I write these last lines. I know I'm saying good-bye to my beloved characters to go on to new stories that are begging to be told, but at the same time, I will miss them dearly.

Graham's story is one I believe we each live in our own way as we grow older and learn the hard, raw truths in life. The challenge of a mother handing over her son to someone she barely knows, the pain of the loss of Tala—these things kill me as I pen them. These people are real to me. I hope you've enjoyed them as much as I have.

There may be a time in the future that I write a sequel, ten years later, to see where those of the next generation find themselves, their challenges and triumphs as life renews the world over.

Some have said the series is far too plausible. It is. Please be careful with our world. Life is fleeting.

Author, A. R. Shaw

Update: The Bitter Earth is now published in the Graham's Resolution series...the story continues.

To be among the first to learn about new releases, announcements, and special projects, please go to AuthorARShaw.com to join my newsletter

Please write a review for *The Last Infidels* on Amazon.com; even a quick word about your experience can be helpful to prospective readers. Click here to write a review.

The author welcomes any comments, feedback, or questions at Annette@AuthorARShaw.com.

BOOKS BY A. R. SHAW

Bite-Sized Offerings

An Anthology Addition

Zombie Mom

ABOUT THE AUTHOR

What the world dreads most has happened...is the tagline AR Shaw writes under and that statement gives you an idea of where her stories often lead...into the abyss of destruction and mayhem with humanity thrown in as a complication. She writes realistic scenarios which are often the worries we think of in the dark of night.

So far she's sold over 51 thousand books and only just begun. AR Shaw resides somewhere in the Pacific Northwest.

f

CPSIA information can be obtained
at www.ICGtesting.com
Printed in the USA
BVHW040302280420
578371BV00015B/747